A COLLISION IN QUEBEC

A COLLISION IN QUEBEC

MICHAEL HARTWIG

Herring Cove Press

Contents

Prologue

My first international voyage was to Quebec City. I was a young boy of nine and traveled with my grandmother from Dallas to Quebec City on a Greyhound bus! My grandmother's nephew (my father's first cousin) from Germany was marrying a beautiful and vivacious French-Canadian woman, and we went for the marriage. I fell in love with Quebec City – with its architecture, with the views of the St. Lawrence River, and with the mystique and charm of people who spoke another language and who had different customs from mine. I believe that first trip out of the United States inspired my love for international travel and languages.

This story flows from that first adventure and countless others over the years. My husband and I travel often to Montreal, Quebec City, and other areas of Quebec with friends. We enjoy exploring neighborhoods, markets, and shops. We often go in the winter to ski and snowshoe.

I want to offer special thanks to Christian Charette, of Provincetown, who is from Quebec and who worked in Morocco as a US diplomat. I appreciate feedback on the plot, help with information about Morocco, and careful attention to French phrases in the narrative.

I also want to thank Frédéric Patenaude, of Montreal, who shares a passion for literature and who has been tutoring me in French for the last couple of years. He provided helpful insights about the plot and characters, has corrected my French, and made helpful suggestions about local expressions and cultural practices.

Another round of thanks goes to Deb Morreale, who read the original manuscript, provided feedback, and inspired the character Deborah in the book.

The story is a work of fiction. Names, characters, businesses, places, events, locales, and incidents are either the products of the author's imagination or used fictitiously.

I hope the story is compelling, romantic, and an enjoyable journey to other worlds. I offer it as a creative way to address the challenges gay people and their families face in the context of religion. It is my belief that whatever God has created (including sexual diversity) is compatible with what God reveals and that the great Abrahamic monotheistic religions – Judaism, Christianity, and Islam – must embrace and affirm gay people and their relationships if they are to be consistent with their own theology and theological methods.

I

Chapter One – Hakim

Hakim merged onto Highway 40 between Montreal and Quebec City, hoping the road crews had done a better job of clearing it than the highway from Sherbrooke. Snow continued to fall heavily, and he wondered if he had made a mistake agreeing to take his passenger to the city. He urgently needed to get supplies to his daughter in nearby Sainte-Marie, so it had made sense earlier.

Brian looked out the window with increased apprehension. Surely it was contrary to statistical probabilities that he would slide off the road twice in one day. He checked the traffic on his phone app. Things were moving. He checked texts, email, and social media as Hakim spoke with someone in Arabic through his earphones.

Hakim finished his conversation and looked over at Brian. "Can you check the traffic?"

Brian nodded. He checked his phone and reported that it was moving. "*C'est fluide.*"

"*La Meteo?*" Hakim asked.

Brian pressed his weather app and opened the radar section. He lifted the phone to Hakim and said, "*Regardez – il y a beaucoup de neige et de glace.*"

"Where is the ice?"

Brian said, "South of here."

Hakim nodded and furrowed his brows as he squinted at the darkening sky outside and tried to keep the car in the grooves made by the traffic in front of him.

Brian felt his heart pound anxiously and his chest tighten as the temperature inside the car rose. He felt nauseous and claustrophobic. A dangling pine air freshener on the rear-view mirror and Hakim's cologne barely concealed the mix of other scents – leather, sweat, and grease - emanating from Hakim's sweatshirt and jacket.

A fast-moving truck passed, throwing wet snow onto the windshield, and causing them to skid slightly. Hakim gripped the wheel of his BMW. Even with the controls set for winter conditions, the traction felt uncertain. He mumbled something in Arabic. Brian mumbled, "Dear God, let us get there safely."

Hakim nodded with a nervous smile. "*Oui – Allah. Dieu et Allah –* the same thing."

Brian nodded.

Hakim asked, "Christian?"

"*Oui. Catholique. Et vous – Musulman?*"

"*Oui, Musulman.*"

A protracted silence followed; a silence Brian associated with his childhood and his father's indifference toward him. He glanced at Hakim to detect whether he might differ from his father – that he might be curious, conversational, light-hearted, or even thoughtful. Unfortunately, he was similarly stern, quiet, and focused on the road, not on light conversation.

Brian sought to engage him, to elicit some warmth and interaction as he had with his own father. "I'm sorry my French is so poor."

Hakim grinned, his white teeth glowing in the dashboard lights. "My English is not that good, either."

"So, you're going to see your daughter?"

"Yes. She and her husband opened a convenience store and gas station. I'm bringing some supplies."

"Do you have any grandchildren?"

"*Pas encore,*" Hakim noted. "They just married in the summer."

Traffic continued to flow despite the intensifying snow and ice. Brian checked the radar again and noticed an ominous line of ice moving toward them. He grew alarmed. He slipped off his coat and gloves and took several deep breaths.

"Wife?" Hakim asked Brian.

Brian held up his hand and presented Hakim with an empty ring finger. "*Pas de femme.*" He wasn't sure if he had just said no wife or no women. In either case, it was correct.

Hakim caught a quick glimpse of Brian's hand and the sheen of the light turquoise polish on his nails. He took a second look. Brian noticed Hakim's shoulders contract and his grip stiffen on the wheel. He wondered if he should have been more discreet.

Hakim raised one of his brows. "*Fiancée? Copine?*"

Brian shook his head no. He had neither a *fiancée* nor a girlfriend.

Hakim grew quiet. He nervously adjusted the windshield wiper speed and the defroster. Distractedly, he played with a few controls on the dashboard. Brian could feel his discomfort.

Hakim shifted subjects. "*Pourquoi le Québec en hiver?*"

Brian and his best friends had always wanted to go to Winter Carnival in Quebec City, an annual celebration of winter with lights, ice sculptures, parades, and outdoor sports. They shared a common passion for skiing and booked an apartment in the historic center of the city with access to excellent restaurants and, of course, cute French Canadian men.

"I'm going to Winter Carnival with friends."

"Ah, yes. Winter Carnival." Hakim paused and then asked, "Where are your friends?"

"New York and Atlanta," Brian responded. "Coming later today."

Hakim shook his head. "I don't think so." He looked out of the window and up toward the sky, implying the conditions were unfavorable for flights.

"Where are you from?" Brian asked Hakim.

"*Maroc.*"

"Ah. Thus, the French."

"*Oui.* And not much English."

"How long have you been in Quebec?"

"My brothers and I came 30 years ago."

"Does everyone work at the garage?" Brian asked, recalling a large contingent of north African men roughly Hakim's age at the place where they towed his car.

Hakim nodded. "But our children marry and start other businesses, like my daughter."

"Thank you for dropping me in the city on your way."

"You're welcome. Buses were canceled and Sherbrooke is boring."

Brian chuckled. "And my car?"

"Ready in a few days. Someone will bring it to you later in the week."

Brian nodded. The thought of his car smashed against a tree haunted him. The black ice came out of nowhere, and he slid uncontrollably toward a ravine.

His phone pinged, and he glanced down at the text from Roberto. "Flights canceled. We'll see about tomorrow. Haven't heard from David and Carlos yet. Presumably they will cancel flights from Atlanta, too."

Roberto was Brian's best friend from New York. They met as undergraduates in Boston at MIT. Roberto went to Columbia for grad school, and Brian remained in Boston, going to Harvard for medical school. Both now worked in medical research. They met David and Carlos in Provincetown several years ago, and they all traveled together now.

"The weather is bad. Take your time," Brian texted back.

"Where are you?" Roberto texted.

"On the highway. Wrecked my car. Garage owner is taking me to Quebec City. Long story. Will fill you in later."

"Oh, my God. Be safe."

Brian looked up. The highway was becoming more treacherous. Snowplows couldn't keep up with the pace of the snow, and freezing rain was mixing in, creating a slippery crust. Hakim shook his head. He leaned forward with an intense gaze to make sure he was in the lane. An accident on the opposite side of the highway snarled traffic for miles. Hakim mumbled something in Arabic.

They approached a convergence of highways and the entrance to the Pierre-Laporte bridge, which crossed the Saint Lawrence River. Hakim slowed as he took the ramp. The snow had reduced traffic on the bridge to one lane in each direction. Hakim's car slid in grooves of the deep snow. He shook his head, and Brian held his breath and gripped the handle on the door as he looked down at the frozen river below.

"Where is your hotel?"

"It's an apartment. On the Rue des Remparts."

Hakim scratched his head and then gripped the steering wheel with both hands. Brian had been to Quebec City only once. He didn't know it well. He looked up the address and asked for directions on his phone. An electronic voice advised them to take the first exit off the bridge and follow the Boulevard Champlain, a road hugging a sliver of land between the river and the cliffs of the upper city. Hakim nodded, indicating he knew the area.

There were fewer cars on the road. Hakim looked nervous as the plows became scarce and the snow heavy. He took the road around the lower part of the city and made his way up a steep ramp, thankfully plowed, and searched for the number of Brian's apartment.

"*Voilà*," he said, looking out of the window at a historic stone building. He pulled to the side but avoided the large banks of snow at the curb. Brian collected his belongings and thanked Hakim. Hakim promised his car would be ready in a few days.

Hakim took out his phone and checked traffic. "*Merde!*" he exclaimed. He then held his hand up to his mouth and uttered, "Sorry."

"What's wrong?" Brian inquired.

"The bridge is closed, and the road going to Sainte-Marie doesn't seem open either."

Brian furrowed his forehead and asked, "Is there another way?"

"No. There's only one bridge."

Hakim looked at the weather app. "*Regardez. Il y a de la glace.*"

Brian looked at Hakim's phone and noticed the large swath of ice falling just south of the river. He realized there was no way Hakim should continue to Sainte-Marie and said, "Hakim, my friends are not coming tonight. Why don't you stay here, and you can leave tomorrow?"

Hakim seemed confused, not sure what Brian had said.

"*Restez ici ce soir*," he explained in French. "There's room."

Hakim seemed hesitant, looked at his phone, and realized he couldn't travel. Reluctantly he said, "*Merci. C'est trop dangereux.*"

"*Oui*," Brian agreed. It was too dangerous.

Hakim looked around and noticed a parking space just up the street. He put the car in gear, inched toward the space, and carefully parked it between several mounds of snow that had been pushed near the curb. He grabbed an overnight bag he had packed for his daughter's and helped Brian unload his suitcase. They walked through the deep snow toward the porch. Brian punched in a code on the door, and it opened. He turned on lights, and Hakim looked around in amazement. Brian had found the apartment online and hoped it would be as nice as the photos. It was a three-bedroom residence with two bathrooms, a modern kitchen, and a spacious parlor with a wood-burning fireplace. He approached the thermostat and kicked on the furnace. The radiators began to creak.

Brian explored the residence while Hakim made a phone call, presumably to his daughter. Brian chose a bedroom and picked another for Hakim. Hakim wandered down the hall after his call and looked in on Brian. Brian said, "Let me show you your room." He walked down the hall and pointed to another bedroom with a bath.

"*Merci.*"

"*Non. Merci à vous.* Thanks for getting us here safe. *Avez-vous faim?*"

Hakim nodded.

"Let's go before the restaurants close."

Hakim and Brian bundled up and walked toward the commercial part of the upper city. Just a few blocks from the apartment, several restaurants and pubs lined Rue Saint-Jean. More than a foot of snow covered the sidewalks. A few lone individuals struggled to clear the walkways with shovels. Around the corner, they found a cozy brasserie. They walked inside, and the server looked at them with chagrin, apparently hoping to close as soon as the remaining patrons had finished their dinners. Brian looked at her with imploring eyes, and she smiled.

Brian had an affable demeanor. The hair on the side of his head was cut short, and he had long wavey tufts of hair on the top, giving him a playful boyish look. His face had a certain elegance and luminosity to it – exuding sophistication and taste. He had sensual lips, a generous and shapely nose, hazel eyes, and a dimple on the right side of his mouth when he smiled. He was of medium height and thin and, although concealed in bulky winter clothing, even Hakim had begun to notice a certain manner of walking – not quite a swish, but close. Brian had a way of extending his shoulder forward and cocking his head slightly back.

"*Un table pour deux, s'il vous plaît,*" Brian implored in his most polite French.

The hostess hesitated, but she melted when Brian batted his thick lashes and smiled.

"*Bien sûr,*" she said, showing them a table.

She observed Hakim carefully, noticing as he removed his hat and coat that he was likely from the Middle East – probably a Muslim. He had dark olive skin, a thin frame, and coarse, dark, short hair. He wore a trimmed beard. He had dark, deeply set eyes and thick brows. He was used to being watched and smiled disarmingly at the waitress.

Brian and Hakim took seats in a wood booth decorated with a few small candles and greenery. The waitress brought them menus and asked what they wanted to drink.

"*Un verre de vin rouge, s'il vous plaît.*" Brian ordered some wine.

"*Un café pour moi,*" Hakim added. As an observant Muslim, he didn't drink.

Brian watched Hakim review the menu, shaking his head.

"What is wrong?" Brian asked in simple English.

"There are limited options for me. I don't eat pork, and other meat must be prepared in a certain way. So, that leaves chicken, and there are debates about whether or not chicken in the Province of Quebec is *halal.*"

"What is *halal?*"

"A proper way of butchering meat. And it must be done by a Muslim or someone of the book – a Jew or a Christian."

"Can you eat vegetarian?"

"Yes, but there aren't good options here," he said as he glanced up and down the menu, slapping the back of his hand dismissively at it. "I think I will trust Allah and have the chicken."

Brian furrowed his brows, wondering if he would offend Hakim if he ordered a hamburger. His wine arrived, and he asked, "Do you mind?"

Hakim shook his head no. "I don't mind the wine and eat whatever you want. It won't bother me."

The waitress returned, looked askance at Hakim, and then smiled at Brian. Brian ordered a burger with fries. Hakim ordered a grilled chicken breast with rice and beans.

Brian lifted his glass to Hakim's coffee and said, "*À votre santé.*" Hakim nodded and said the same.

Hakim wrung his hands nervously, searching for something to talk about. "So, where are you from?"

"Boston."

"Did you grow up there?"

"No. My parents live in Georgia. And you, you live in Sherbrooke?" Brian inquired.

"Yes. With my family."

"Wife and children?"

"Yes. One daughter in Sainte-Marie and one son who helps at the garage when he's not in school."

"And you are from Morocco?"

Hakim nodded proudly.

"Are there many from Morocco in Quebec?" Brian didn't associate a large northern African immigrant population with Quebec and wondered if Hakim was an anomaly or part of a larger demographic shift.

Hakim nodded. "Yes, there are quite a few." Then he asked abruptly, "How old are you?"

"Thirty."

"*Et pas de femme?*"

Brian shuffled in his seat and cleared his throat. Hakim was an observant Muslim. He wasn't sure he wanted to share that he was gay, but it was difficult to conceal his painted nails and Hakim had probably already noticed the flair with which he spoke and waved his hands.

"*Non, pas de femme.*"

Hakim was curious and pressed Brian. "Why not?"

"School and work," he replied evasively. Hakim's curiosity about his marital status unnerved him.

Hakim raised one of his eyebrows. He detected Brian's insincerity. He opened his phone and scrolled through photos. "Here is my wife, Aisha. And this is my daughter, Jamila," he said proudly. He smiled radiantly as Brian looked at the photos.

"She's beautiful," Brian noted.

"And your son?" Brian asked.

Reluctantly, Hakim scrolled through some photos and pulled up a picture of his son. "This is Yusef."

Adorable, Yusef had expressive dark eyes, a warm smile, a long sexy nose, and sensual lips. He looked like he was 16 or 17. Brian gasped for air, and he feared Hakim noticed. Hakim pulled the phone back from Brian.

Their meals arrived, and Hakim voiced a blessing in Arabic and began to cut the chicken. Brian picked up the burger in his hand and bit into the juicy meat.

Brian looked over Hakim's shoulder and out of the front window. A few lonely souls passing on the walkway shielded themselves from the fiercely blowing snow. Hakim consumed the chicken with abandon, and Brian savored the crispy fries.

"Why did you come to Canada?" Brian asked Hakim.

"Hm," Hakim murmured, not sure where to start. "Opportunity."

Brian nodded at the familiar refrain of immigrants to the US and Canada. *"Pas d'opportunités au Maroc?"*

"Well, there's opportunity as long as you don't offend certain people. I don't know the entire story, but someone in the Moroccan government helped us immigrate. Perhaps my father knew something or had done something that required our leaving."

"That's too bad. I'm sure you miss your home."

Hakim looked off into the distance with longing. "Yes. I do. Particularly on a night like this."

"I can imagine. You've come to one of the coldest places to live."

"It was easier to get into Canada than the US. There's more acceptance here and easier immigration rules."

Brian nodded and wondered if Hakim noticed the irony of his own statement, a devout Muslim sitting across from an irreligious gay man.

They continued to visit and eat. The restaurant had emptied, and the staff were already cleaning the bar area in preparation for closing.

"Are you ready to head back?" Brian asked Hakim as they finished the last bites of their food.

"Oui. I want to do my prayers."

Brian paid the tab, and they bundled up for the short walk home. Once inside the warm apartment, Hakim retreated to his room, pulled out a prayer rug he had brought in from the car, and prostrated himself toward Mecca. Brian finished unpacking. He brought a bottle of wine from his suitcase into the kitchen, opened it, and poured a generous glass for himself. He went into the parlor, lit the kindling under several logs in the fireplace, and watched the flames singe the resin of the wood as they began to burn.

A few minutes later, Hakim joined him. "Do you want some water or tea?" Brian inquired.

Hakim nodded. "Tea, please."

They sat together on the sofa, facing the fire. Hakim had some prayer beads he thumbed, mumbling prayers under his breath. He looked over at Brian, lifted the beads in his hand, and said, "You don't mind?"

Brian nodded no, oddly comforted by the orange flames in the fireplace, the velvety red wine, and the soothing cadence of Hakim's quiet prayers.

"It's Sunday. You don't pray?" Hakim inquired.

Brian nodded no.

"*Pourquoi?*"

Brian hesitated, unsure whether he wanted to get into a theological discussion with Hakim. Hakim leaned forward, eager for Brian to answer.

"Religion is a problem," Brian said as simply as possible.

Hakim furrowed his forehead, eager for Brian to elaborate.

"Hatred, wars, abuse."

"But your religion says God is love. You must love."

"Yes," Brian began, "but my religion doesn't love me."

Hakim shook his head as if bewildered.

Brian cleared his throat and said timidly, "I am gay. The priest says I am bad. My parents threw me out of the house because they say I am a sinner - that I am evil." A tear ran down Brian's cheek.

Hakim became visibly tense and furrowed his brows. He paused his prayers. He leaned forward and said, "God is merciful."

"I don't need mercy," Brian said sternly, in retort.

"God created man and woman for love," Hakim added, quoting the Qur'an. "You will find a good woman you can love and fulfill God's commands."

"I've tried. It's not fair to the woman."

"God, who is merciful, will change you."

"No. God won't and hasn't changed me."

Hakim didn't reply. He remained quiet, stewing in his thoughts. He was snowbound with Brian, and it troubled him. He abstained from alcohol, ate only *halal* food, and said his prayers faithfully. Now he was seated across from a gay man.

"*Excusez moi. Je vais me coucher,*" Hakim said, taking his leave of Brian and heading back to his room.

Brian wished him a good night. "*Bonne nuit.*"

Hakim merely nodded.

"Well, that went well," Brian mumbled to himself.

He quickly called Roberto. "Hello! Brian, how's it going?" Roberto answered.

"Horrible. I had a wreck on the way here, and one of the owners of the garage drove me to Quebec City. The roads are closed, so he's stuck here – and he's a fundamentalist Muslim."

"Is he cute?"

"Roberto! Are you kidding?"

"I've always fantasized about doing it with a handsome Arab. They're so hot!"

"And bigoted."

"Not all of them."

"This one is. I hope the roads are clear tomorrow. Any word on the flights?"

"David and Carlos are stuck in Atlanta. The airline says they will let us know tomorrow morning of the revised schedule. Fortunately, there are seats available once flights resume. By the way, how's the apartment?"

"Beautiful. You'll love it."

"Can't wait. Let's talk tomorrow."

"*Ciao,*" Brian said.

"*Ciao, bello,*" Roberto replied.

Brian pressed an app on his phone to see what kind of hook-ups there might be nearby. Quebec City wasn't known as a party town, but given the large university, he was hoping he would meet some hot local guys. He was always partial to French Canadian men - dark hair, large sensual noses, olive complexion, and their sexy accents. He looked forward to snuggling up with one in front of a roaring fireplace while it snowed outside. A few handsome guys popped up on the screen, one of them only a block away. He was tempted, but decided he had enough adventure for one day. "Tomorrow," he murmured to himself. He drank his wine and waited for the fire to die down. Once the embers were quiet, he went to his room, washed up, stripped, and slid under the soft duvet, and fell quickly asleep.

2

Chapter Two – Exploring Quebec City

Brian woke to the sound of a snowplow passing along the roadway outside the residence. He walked to the window, pulled back the curtains, and noticed the snow continuing to fall. Drifts of snow reached to the base of the windows. The overnight storm buried cars and walkways, and the front garden was a sea of white.

Brian walked down the hall toward the kitchen and noticed Hakim doing his prayers in his room. The landlord had left coffee and filters, but Brian realized they had nothing to eat. He made coffee and sipped it pensively. Hakim wandered into the parlor and said, "Too much snow. Roads are still closed."

It didn't surprise Brian. "Coffee?"

Hakim nodded. Brian poured him a cup, and they sat silently at the table.

"I'll go get us something to make breakfast," Brian offered.

"I will come with you," Hakim replied. He was restless and wanted to get out of the house.

Brian nodded. Brian searched for a market on his phone. "*Il y a une épicerie près d'ici*," Brian noted as he located one nearby on his phone map.

Hakim put on his coat. Near the front door, they found a couple of snow shovels. They pushed the door open against the drift of snow on the porch and shoveled their way to the street. The street was deep with snow, but more passible than the walkways. Old stone homes lined the narrow lanes. Heavy snow curved over the edge of the rooftops and frosted the colorful shutters framing the windows. Blowing snow made visibility difficult as both leaned into the wind and made their way uphill toward Rue Saint-Jean.

Brian and Hakim trudged past shops, mostly dark and shuttered for the storm. They finally arrived at the *épicerie* and pushed their way through the front door. They shook snow off their coats and looked around. The market was a classic neighborhood store with fresh vegetables, fruit, prepared dinners, spices, bread, cheeses, beverages, and a butcher. They grabbed a basket and wove their way through the narrow aisles jammed with people getting provisions to endure what seemed like an interminable storm. Brian picked up fruit, salad, soup, pasta, sauce, cheese, crackers, pastries, and wine. Both he and Hakim walked to the meat section and noticed several labels with *halal* certification. Hakim's eyes widened in delight and looked at Brian, who nodded for him to pick up several steaks. They paid the cashier and returned home.

Once inside the apartment, Brian asked, "Would you like a croissant and marmalade?"

Hakim nodded.

"And fruit?" Brian added.

Hakim poured them each another cup of coffee, and they sat looking out the window at the white tempest outside.

"Will the roads reopen?" Brian asked nervously.

Hakim looked doubtful, shaking his head. "We will see. This is a severe storm."

Brian sighed, wondering what he and Hakim would do to pass the time. "Should we take a walk?" he asked.

Hakim seemed eager to do something and nodded excitedly.

"Do you know the city?" Brian inquired.

"A little. I'll give you a tour. *On y va?*"

"*Oui.* Let's go."

Brian stood, emptied his coffee mug, and retreated to his bathroom, washed his face, and brushed his teeth. A while later, they gathered in the parlor and bundled up for their excursion.

The snow continued to fall, but less forcefully. They walked out the front door, down the street, and down a steep road toward the Rue Saint-Paul. It was a historic lane lined with antique shops, galleries, cafes, and restaurants. The storefronts were old, with decorative wood trim painted in bright colors. Shop owners were shoveling snow, and a few intrepid souls were out looking for coffee, pastries, and supplies.

Brian savored the salutations neighbors exchanged with one another as they cleared the walkways – a *bonjour* here and a *comment ça va* there. He loved stepping into another world – a simpler way of life organized around urban neighborhoods, local cafes, and small shops. He smelled the aroma of freshly roasted coffee near a shop window filled with burlap bags of coffee bean and a roaster churning inside.

Several galleries showcased local artists. Brian noted the use of bright colors, undoubtedly a way to brighten long gray winters. An image of a winter scene caught his eye. He lingered in front of the window and felt Hakim's impatient stare, beckoning him to continue. It was too cold to linger long in one place.

Hakim led them down the Rue Saint-Paul to an intersection

of roads. They turned right toward a pedestrian zone - the Rue du Sault-au-Matelot - set between modest size apartment buildings with more shops, galleries, and restaurants on the street level. Many establishments had affixed elaborate planters on the window ledges filled with winter greens, decorative birch logs, and curly twigs of various hues and textures. Multihued lights cascaded out of the planters, creating a colorful, luminescent effect on the fresh snow.

"It's so beautiful and festive," Brian remarked, his head pivoting back and forth at the winter beauty laid out before him.

Hakim nodded. The compact walled city of Quebec reminded him of his home in Morocco, where whitewashed buildings lined small walkways and protected inhabitants from the intense heat of the summer. He thought it ironic that he was living now in one of the coldest parts of the world.

"It's so cold here. Couldn't your father have gone someplace else?" Brian remarked.

"Maybe. But life here is good. We adapt."

Brian wondered how adaptable Hakim really was given his religious and cultural sentiments. They continued their walk into the oldest part of Quebec City, a plaza surrounded by 17th century stone manors and a historic church, Our Lady of Victories. Brian pivoted in place, taking in the venerable stone buildings laden with snow. This was the original center of the oldest settlement of Quebec City in the 1600s. Over the years, it had suffered fires, reconstruction, abandonment, and finally restoration as a symbol of Quebec's heritage.

There was a large evergreen tree standing in the center of the square surrounded by elaborate ice sculptures created for the Winter Carnival. People gathered in the square, observing the sculptures, and eating maple syrup snow cones sold at a rustic wooden booth. Children screamed as they threw snowballs at each other. Brian was surprised that people were out in the snow and cold but realized this was the whole point of Winter Carnival - to embrace winter and have fun.

Brian and Hakim stood in the square and observed the festive activity. Brian's wide eyes and enthusiasm encouraged Hakim, who said, "Come, I will show you the Petit-Champlain!"

They walked around the corner of the church and onto another small lane that led from the river to a long cluster of buildings built near and under the massive cliffs rising to the upper city. A beautiful funicular rose vertically nearby. Lights in the windows of the shops created a warm yellow glow on the fresh snow. More lights were strung between buildings over the walkway and each shop decorated window boxes and entry ways with greenery.

Brian's eyes widened at the winter paradise. It was the quintessential charming old-world lane filled with cozy boutiques and people wrapped in chic winter attire wandering in and out of the shops. Hakim looked proudly at Brian, who stopped at each store and looked in the windows at clothing, housewares, and pastry.

They approached a small brasserie, and Brian said, "Shall we go in and get something to drink or eat? I'm cold."

Hakim nodded, rubbing his hands on his upper arms to generate warmth.

A server welcomed them. Hakim asked for a table, but none were available. The server suggested a couple of seats at the bar, and Hakim nodded.

They took seats, and Brian said, "This is so charming." He looked across the bar through large windows facing the Saint Lawrence River, full of ice and snow.

"*Oui, charmant.* It's not like this in Sherbrooke. Quebec City has preserved its history and architecture. I like it here."

"Me, too. Thanks for showing me around. Are you okay sitting at the bar?"

"*Pas de problème,*" Hakim assured him, seemingly at ease with the alcohol around him.

The bartender gave them menus. Hakim ordered an herbal tea, and Brian a glass of wine. As the bartender poured his glass, Brian caught the eye of a guy across from them, who smiled warmly. He sat between several friends chatting, but noticed Brian as he removed his coat, scarf, and hat.

Hakim noticed the exchange and looked uncomfortable. He buried his face in the menu, but looked up occasionally as Brian and the man exchanged glances. Hakim mumbled something in Arabic. Brian felt it must have been a disparaging remark, given Hakim's body language and grimace.

Hakim ordered a vegetarian pizza, and Brian ordered a classic Parisienne sandwich - French bread, ham, butter, and cornichons. Their meals came, and the man across from them raised his glass toward Brian, no longer concealing his interest. Hakim feared he would be pegged as a gay friend, and scooted farther away, slightly turning his back away from Brian.

The guy was handsome. He had short dark hair, a typical large French nose, red sensual lips, and a warm smile. Brian was intrigued, looking over at him from time to time. Hakim became more irritated and said, "Why do you insult Allah?"

The critical remark took Brian by surprise. "How is my behavior an insult to God?" he replied defensively.

"Man with man is not natural. God says it is wrong in the Qur'an and in the Bible."

"It's natural to me," Brian responded.

"No," Hakim responded. "You just think it is."

"No. I have tried to change."

"*Pas possible,*" Hakim continued in French. "If you pray to Allah, you will change."

"I have prayed. There is no change."

Hakim shook his head. "You don't go to church. You don't pray. Allah is merciful, but Allah wants devotion."

Brian felt blood rush to his face and his pulse raced as adrenaline coursed through his body. Hakim's words touched raw nerves. He had grown up in a devout Catholic family, and he was active in the church, the conscientious boy, excelling in Sunday school and leading his confirmation class in memorizing the catechism. When he first detected his attraction to men, he confessed it regularly, and he prayed he would change. Nothing changed. When he was in high school, the feelings intensified, and he became despondent, even suicidal. His parents paid for counseling, but his attraction to men only increased.

During his junior year in high school, he dated a classmate. His parents found out and gave him an ultimatum. He could cease what they considered foolishness and perversion, or he would have to leave home. He chose to leave. His boyfriend's parents took him in. The two classmates became companions instead of lovers, and Brian finished school and went off to college.

"Why would I go to a church that hates me? I love God, but God's people didn't love me."

Hakim looked perturbed. "They only wanted what is good for you. If you are cast off from God, only bad will happen."

"I'm not cast off from God. I'm cast off from hateful people."

Hakim shook his head and finished his pizza. Brian gulped down the rest of his wine and indicated he was ready to leave. They paid their tab, put on their coats, and walked toward the door. The guy at the bar hopped up and approached Brian with a slip of paper. "*Mon numéro,*" he said, winking at Brian.

Brian nodded, smiled, and folded it into one of his pockets. He and Hakim walked out into the snow and retraced steps toward the funicular. Brian wanted a graceful way to excuse himself. Hakim's religious fundamentalism was ruining his vacation. Hakim seemed annoyed, too. He was quiet and withdrawn, but his cultural background mandated hospitality – making sure the stranger was safe and taken care of. Looking at the funicular, Hakim reluctantly said, "Shall we take this up?"

Brian hesitated, pondering how he might come up with a pretext to go the other way. He, too, felt some sense of responsibility to accommodate Hakim, who had been so generous in bringing him to the city. He also didn't want to piss him off, jeopardizing the repair of his car. "Sure. Where does this take us?"

"To the upper city, to your apartment and the nearby Chateau Frontenac."

They entered, paid for tickets, and stepped into the cabin of the funicular. A few other tourists entered the space. The doors closed, and the lift began to ascend the steep incline. Brian's face was glued to the window as the cabin rose over frosty slate roofs of the lower city and the St. Lawrence River in the near distance. The views were amazing even with the low clouds and falling snow. At the terminus, they exited onto a plaza in front of the majestic hotel, a historic structure that resembled a medieval French castle. The heavy snow concealed the upper turrets, shrouded in an ominous fog.

Fortunately, the wind had calmed. Hakim waved Brian forward to the boardwalk and terrace, taking in the panoramic views of the river. Large chunks of ice floated by, occasionally broken by the passenger ferry taking workers back and forth from Lévis to Quebec City. Downstream, Brian made out the outlines of a bridge to an island in the middle of the river. To the right, a steep toboggan track lined with bright lights rose above the boardwalk. People screamed as their sleds sped down the track of ice and came to a halt in front of a crowd of observers.

Hakim pointed out landmarks, and Brian nodded quietly, still nursing resentment at Hakim's earlier remarks. Hakim picked up on Brian's mood and shifted the conversation. He asked, "What do you do for a living?"

"I am a research scientist."

Hakim furrowed his brows as if he didn't understand.

"Medicine. Science," Brian stated more simply.

"Doctor?"

Brian nodded since technically he was a doctor, but he worked primarily in pharmaceutical research.

Hakim seemed impressed, rubbing his chin thoughtfully. "How?"

"What do you mean, how?"

"Your parents kicked you out of your home. How did you become a doctor?" Hakim turned toward Brian, conveying a genuine interest in knowing more.

"It wasn't easy," Brian replied. "I was determined to fulfill my dreams even if I didn't have their support. Between scholarships and work, I managed."

"Impressive," Hakim remarked as he glanced pensively over the view of the river below.

"Boyfriend?" Hakim asked awkwardly, pushing past his comfort zone.

Hakim touched a raw nerve. "No."

"Why not?"

"*C'est une longue histoire,*" Brian said in French, surprised he recalled the appropriate words to say, 'a long story.'

"*J'ai le temps,*" Hakim stated matter-of-factly, not having anything else to do.

Brian was surprised by Hakim's declared interest in hearing more. He squinted his eyes in disbelief, and Hakim raised his brows in defiance.

"*Un café?*" Brian offered. They had just had lunch, but it was too cold to stand or sit outside, and the warm lights of the Chateau Frontenac promised a nice place to warm up and chat.

"*Un chocolat chaud, peut-être.*" Hakim looked toward the massive structure of the hotel. "I'm cold. Shall we go inside?"

Brian nodded, and they walked toward the hotel. They entered the lobby, an opulent old-world space with well-heeled clientele on winter holiday. Brian asked the concierge if there was a café inside, and the individual pointed down the hall. Brian led Hakim through the gallery of shops to a cozy coffee shop. They took seats, and an attractive woman approached.

"*Qu'est-ce que je peux vous servir?*"

"*Un double espresso pour moi et un chocolat chaud pour lui,*" Brian ordered.

The server brought their drinks. Hakim stirred the hot chocolate, and Brian sipped his double espresso. "You were going to tell me your story," Hakim reminded him, looking over the edge of his cup of chocolate as he took a first sip.

Brian was hesitant, but felt he had nothing to lose recounting a painful chapter in his life. "Well," he began tentatively. "In college, I met a classmate, and we fell in love."

Hakim bristled, took another long sip of his beverage, and breathed deeply.

Brian wondered if he should continue. Hakim nodded to him to continue. "We finished college. I went to graduate school and Eric found a job in Boston."

Hakim stared at Brian stoically.

"We were happy. We bought a condo, made friends, got a dog, and had a pleasant life."

"What happened?"

"A few years later, Eric fell in love with someone else."

"But how?" Hakim inquired, assuming amongst gay men, Brian would have been a catch. After all, he was attractive, affable, and a doctor.

"He said he never loved me."

"How is that possible?"

Brian was surprised by Hakim's question. He wondered if he might not be capable of sympathy or compassion after all? He took a deep breath and continued. "That's what I asked, too. How do you share a home and life for several years, and then suddenly your partner says, I don't love you; I didn't love you?"

Hakim was moved by Brian's story. He knew a few gay clients and vendors but had always kept his distance, never wanting to know much about their personal lives. The challenges Brian had faced were formidable, and Hakim began to reconsider his initial impressions.

"Since then?"

"No one. I guess I'm gun shy."

Hakim furrowed his brows, not understanding the phrase.

"I don't trust anyone."

"Oh. *Je comprends. Je suis désolé.*"

"*Merci,*" Brian replied.

They continued to visit, searching for less controversial topics like travel and sports. Brian was a fan of the Boston Bruins, and Hakim liked hockey. Hakim enjoyed travel and went to New York whenever he could. He was full of contrasts – a garage owner who had gone to private school as a kid and who could spend hours in the Met looking at classic works of art. He liked opera, musicals, and poking around in independent bookstores. Brian wondered if there wasn't a back story somewhere.

They finished their beverages and looked out the large window. The snow had slowed to flurries. Hakim took out his phone, looked up the traffic, and said, "The bridge is still closed. I'll have to wait a little longer. I don't want to take up your time."

"*Ne vous inquietez pas* - don't worry," Brian said, though still hoping for some solitude when Hakim would eventually leave for his daughter's home.

"Shall we go back to the apartment and see if the roads open later? Maybe we can relax or watch television."

Hakim nodded. They took a leisure stroll back to the apartment. Peaks of sun glistened on the irregular surface of the snow. Shadows of purple, blue, and turquoise on the piles of snow looked like an impressionist painting. They passed the cathedral and the old seminary, a classic French-style stone building and courtyard surrounded by a tall decorative iron fence.

Brian loved winter. He loved the sound of snow squeaking under boots, the piles shoveled on the side of walkways, and boughs of evergreens heavily laden after a storm. People were now darting in and out of shops, wrapped in heavy coats, scarfs, hats, and mittens. Brian made a mental note of several clothing stores he wanted to visit later in the week.

Once inside the apartment, Hakim retreated to his room to pray, and Brian sat in the parlor, checking emails and a dating app to see if there were any prospects for the evening.

Roberto texted: "Looks like flights will resume tomorrow. We'll let you know when we should arrive."

Brian replied: "Great. You might want to rent a car until mine is fixed."

"Will do," Roberto responded.

"And David and Carlos?"

"They're arriving sometime tomorrow as well."

"I can't wait," Brian typed in, using a few emojis to express his excitement.

The sky was darkening, and a second round of snow began. Brian looked at the weather app and noticed one last band of moderate snow. Hakim walked down the hall toward the parlor.

"My daughter says the roads are still closed, but the snow is winding down, and they hope to have them open this evening. I will leave soon."

"Why don't we make dinner, and then we can check conditions later?"

"*D'accord*. I'll help," Hakim offered, smiling warmly.

Brian went into the kitchen and surveyed pots, pans, and equipment they would need. They had two *halal* steaks, and Brian thought a steak-au-poivre might be appropriate in Quebec. He found some brandy, peppercorns, and other ingredients. Hakim said cooking down the brandy would be religiously acceptable. He offered to make salad and a Moroccan couscous with ingredients they had picked up at the *épicerie*.

Once ready, they sat at the dining table. Hakim had a glass of water and Brian a glass of wine. They clinked glasses and cut into the tender steak.

"*Ah, c'est bon!*" Hakim began.

"*Oui, et j'aime le couscous.*"

"*Merci. Et merci pour votre hospitalité.*" Hakim had grown more comfortable with Brian, who seemed respectful and thoughtful, even if he was gay. He looked up as he cut his steak and asked, "You mentioned your parents threw you out of the house. How is that possible?"

The question threw Brian off-guard. He imagined Hakim would be fully capable of throwing Yusef out of the house or out of the business if he found he was dating a male classmate or someone in town. He took a sip of wine and replied, "In all honesty, I don't know. How could a parent do that?"

"*Oui, vraiment.* It's unimaginable," Hakim said pensively, rubbing his chin.

"But if you felt like Allah wanted you to do it, would you?"

Brian's question startled Hakim, who tensed up. He thought of himself as a devout Muslim, one who "submits" to God. God demands obedience. Some jurists pondered the appropriate response to men who had sex with men. Since the story of Sodom described

God casting fire and brimstone on the inhabitants of the town that sought to rape the angelic visitors, there were some Muslim jurists who felt capital punishment was the right response to homosexuals. Hakim couldn't imagine killing his son or nephews, but he could imagine casting them out of the family circle.

Brian detected Hakim's dilemma and added, "If Yusef was gay, how would you handle it?"

"He's not."

"But if for some reason he was, and he tried to change, but couldn't, what would you do? Would you be okay not seeing him for the rest of your life? Like my parents?"

Hakim pondered what Brian said and realized how agonizing it must have been for Brian and for his parents. They were estranged, and they have had no contact over the years. What must it have been like for Brian at 17 to have been abandoned, shunned, cast off and to have to forge a life without his parents or their support? What would it be like for parents to ignore their son forever? It was unimaginable. He thought of his wife, Aisha, and realized her heart would break if she had to cast her son off. Surely there must be another way to reconcile Islam with a gay son or daughter.

"I can't imagine throwing a child out. Family is too important."

"More important than Islam?" Brian asked pointedly.

Hakim rubbed his hand through his hair nervously and then cut another piece of meat, delaying his response as long as possible. He stared at Brian and said thoughtfully, "I'm not a scholar. I suppose there must be some way. And you, have you found a way to reconcile Christianity with your identity?"

"I used to think that was important – that it was crucial for me to reconcile my orientation with Christianity or with the Catholic Church. I felt that loyalty to God meant being loyal to my religion. If I gave up on the religion, I was giving up on God. But then I realized God and religion are not the same. Religion is a way of pointing to God, but it isn't God. I've grown to appreciate that being loyal to God is being loyal to God's creation and respecting what God has created – including sexual diversity, the environment, and other people."

Hakim nodded pensively. He paused and then said, "*Ça suffit.* Enough religion. Let's just enjoy our meal."

Brian welcomed the reprieve, took a sip of his wine, and finished the remaining portion of couscous. "Delicious."

"Yes. It was good." Hakim folded the napkin on his lap and reached for his phone. He checked traffic and smiled. "It looks like the bridge has opened and traffic is moving."

"I'm sure you are eager to get to your daughter. Will you be okay on the road?"

He nodded. He stood, took dishes to the sink, and then walked back to the room to retrieve his prayer rug and coat.

"*Brian, c'etait un honneur de faire votre connaissance.*"

"*Moi aussi,*" Brian said, agreeing with Hakim's sentiments about the fortuitousness of their meeting. He shook Hakim's hand warmly.

Surprisingly, Hakim reached his arms around Brian and gave him an embrace. He put on his coat, hat, and gloves and walked out onto the porch. A few errant flurries caught the porch light as Hakim walked toward his car. Brian helped him clear it and waved as he drove off.

Brian returned to the apartment, stripped Hakim's bed, and threw the sheets in the washer. He returned to the parlor, threw some logs in the fireplace, and lit them. He sat on the sofa and watched the flames begin to consume the wood.

"What an unexpected twenty-four hours," he murmured to himself. He cocked his head in thought, wondering if meeting Hakim was anything more than a random event. How did the universe throw such diverse people together? They were two souls inhabiting radically different worlds yet forced to share time and food and conversation. What were the odds?

3

Chapter Three – Rendezvous

Brian reached into his pocket and pulled out the small piece of paper with a phone number and the name 'Bastien.' He dialed the number.

"*Allô*," a man with deep voice and luscious French accent responded.

"*Allô, Je suis Brian, l'homme au bar cet après midi.*"

"*Ah, oui.* I'm glad you called. I'm Bastien," he said, shifting to English after noting Brian's accent.

"I'm here on vacation. I was wondering if you might like to come over for a glass of wine," Brian offered awkwardly. They had only exchanged eye contact, so there wasn't much to build a conversation on. He was used to being direct with hookups.

There was hesitation on the other end of the line. Bastien cleared his throat. "You were with someone this afternoon. You're not looking for a threesome, are you?"

"God, no! That was someone who was repairing my car, and we were getting a bite to eat."

"Ah," Bastien replied, relieved. "Where are you?"

"Rue des Remparts."

"I'm nearby."

Brian gave him the number of the apartment, and Bastien said he would be right over. Brian straightened the living room, went to the bathroom, freshened up, and put on a new sweater that was loose and easy to remove. He looked in the mirror and smiled at himself.

His heart raced in anticipation. He loved the thrill of someone new. A bit of danger, intrigue, and longing. The foreign element heightened the excitement – a greater sense of vulnerability around language and customs. It was also the perfect antidote to monotony, the exploration of novel physical features of local men, discovering new expressions and words, and immersing oneself in another world.

A few minutes later, Bastien knocked on the door. Brian opened it and waved Bastien inside. "Let me take your coat," he said, as Bastien began to unwrap his scarf, remove his hat and gloves, and take off his coat. Brian breathed in Bastien's cologne, a subtle but distinct fragrance, one not common in Boston.

"Nice place," Bastien remarked, looking around the room.

"It's a rental. My friends and I have it for the week."

Bastien scrutinized the place with a worried look.

"Don't worry. They're not here. They're delayed because of the storm. They won't get here until tomorrow."

Bastien raised his brows, realizing his good fortune.

"Do you want some wine?"

"Isn't that why you invited me?" Bastien said playfully, winking at Brian.

"*C'est un apero,*" Brian said, suggesting it was just foretaste to something that would follow. He uncorked the bottle of red.

"*J'ai déjà mangé*," Bastien interjected playfully as Brian began to pour the wine.

"Maybe, but did you already have desert?" Brian replied, handing him a generous glass of wine.

"*Pas encore*," Bastien said, grinning and lifting his glass to Brian's.

"*Santé*," they both said in unison.

"Where are you from?" Bastien began.

"Boston."

"You seem to have a good command of French," Bastien said with a look of surprise.

"I manage."

"Boston's a beautiful city," Bastien added.

"Yes. I like it. Quebec City is equally beautiful, particularly in the winter."

"Are you here for Winter Carnival?"

"Yes. My friends and I were planning to ski. The storm has delayed things a bit."

"My luck," Bastien grinned. He approached Brian and gave him a kiss. He found Brian adorable. He loved the playfulness of his hair, the luminescence of his face, and the grace of his body. He had a warm smile and a cute dimple on one side of his mouth.

Brian rubbed his hands over Bastien's shoulder and down his arm, squeezing his biceps. Bastien was imposing – tall and muscular. He had broad shoulders and a well-built chest. Brian rubbed his hands over Bastien's pecs and said, "You must work out."

"From time to time," Bastien said, blushing. He set his wine glass down and reached his arms around Brian, squeezing Brian's round buttocks.

"I like a guy who knows what he wants," Brian said, giving Bastien a long, moist kiss. He took Bastien's hands and led him to the sofa, pushing him down on the cushions and straddling him with his legs.

"*Moi aussi*," Bastien remarked, gazing into Brian's eyes hovering over him.

Brian liked to take control. He was turned on by the mystique of a new trick, the challenge of navigating a new body and decrypting its secrets. He had perfected the art of deflection, keeping his lovers in the dark, erecting a thick shield around his emptiness and pain.

Brian began to unbutton Bastien's sweater, slipping his warm hand in the loose opening of the shirt underneath. Bastien leaned his head back and moaned. Brian traced his hands around the firm muscles of Bastien's chest, feeling the soft dark hair. He could feel himself becoming aroused.

Bastien reached up and unzipped Brian's pants, slipping his hand up under the leg of Brian's undershorts and feeling his hard shaft. He stroked it a few times and then withdrew his hand, rubbing it along Brian's back, and smiled. "*Bien amanché*. Well endowed! Hm."

Bastien noticed Brian's painted nails and was intrigued by his exaggerated gestures. He thought Brian might be fragile, a bit effeminate, a bottom. In actuality, Brian's dress and mannerisms were a long-cultivated protest and cover for having to conform. When Bastien felt Brian's long hard shaft and peered into his piercing hazel eyes, he began to reassess his date and realized he was in for a rough ride.

They continued to undress each other with abandon, exploring the contours of each other's bodies. The embers of the fire were glowing orange, casting a soft radiance around the room. Their bodies glistened with perspiration as they grew increasingly aroused.

Brian kissed Bastien's ripped abdomen. His caramel skin was smooth and glistened in the ambient light. It had a distinctive flavor, sweet and spicy, almost as if it were a mix of crème brûlée and toasted coffee. He nuzzled his nose in the soft hair covering Bastien's pecs and could feel his own erection throbbing as it grazed Bastien's below him.

Bastien leaned his head back as Brian licked his neck and clavicle. The weight and solidity of Brian on top of him felt exhilarating, a turning of tables. He was used to taking control, but he relished Brian's famished lips devouring him. Bastien ran his hands over Brian's shoulders and down his side, grabbing hold of his firm buttocks and pulling Brian tightly against him. He nuzzled his hardness between Brian's legs. He could feel the heat of Brian's shaft burn against his stomach.

Although strangers, their bodies found a common language, quickly making sense of each other's preferences. Being of the same gender, they needed little coaching to know what the other liked or how to make things work. Brian and Bastien quickly fell into sync, knowing just where to stroke, just how to kiss, and the precise moment to pull back to intensify craving.

Brian rubbed his hands through Bastien's dark, silky hair. He peered into his deep-set eyes, searching for a narrative, for a story to latch onto, a world to travel to if only for a few moments. They kissed deeply, savoring the fusing of their breath as each welcomed the other in.

Bastien rarely pursued Americans. He found them unimaginative and lacking in sophistication and style. Sitting near the exotic Hakim at the bar, Bastien thought Brian was European, perhaps someone from Italy or Austria. He was intrigued by his hair, the playfulness of his eyes, and cut of his clothes. He was charmed with Brian's French and elated Brian didn't lack for creativity as he took possession of Bastien's body. Bastien pressed his hardness deeper into the folds of Brian's buttocks, letting the mounting moistness lubricate him. He could feel himself throb in anticipation as Brian flexed around his sex.

Bastien's body - hard, firm, and taut – fed Brian's craving for vitality and strength. He rode the force of Bastien's muscles flexed against his own and savored the flow of blood filing his veins and hardening his cock. He pressed against Bastien, who, with equal force, resisted. Their bodies forestalled the awaited culmination as long as possible, clinging to the intense craving coursing through them.

Bastien closed his eyes and felt the union of their bodies, no longer alien or unacquainted but now kin, familiar, intimate. It was the antidote to the void he often felt as a single gay man who had never found the one. For a fleeting moment, he felt the powerful rush of warmth and affection. Loneliness and self-doubt gave way to the person on top of him, consuming him and filling deep cavities with presence and hoped for companionship.

Bastien opened his eyes, and Brian could feel the camaraderie of the exchange, two *gamins* who had created imaginary worlds and had invited each other to play. Surprisingly, they could speak each other's invented languages, and knew the position of the soldiers on the battlefield as they prepared for the next offensive.

Brian felt the heat of Bastien's skin pressed against his own and sensed the escalating ardor ready to erupt. He could delay their release no longer and felt waves of intense pleasure race through him. He watched Bastien's face tighten, then relax, slipping into his own state of repose and contentment. They both clung to the fleeting arousal, gripping each other's skin in soft but strong hands.

Brian collapsed on Bastien's chest, listening to his heart pound, and feeling his chest rise and fall with each breath. Bastien's hand on his back felt comforting, a gesture of affection when both knew they were on the verge of retreat, a withdrawal into their own safe worlds. He lifted his head, gave Bastien a kiss, and stood up. He wiped himself with his tee-shirt and put on his shorts. He sat back down on the sofa, pressing his buttocks next to Bastien, who was stretched out on the cushions.

"Wow!" Brian said. "I heard the French Canadians were good, but you have far exceeded expectations."

"You're not bad yourself. Even for an American!"

They both chuckled. Bastien leaned forward and slid to the side of the sofa, pulling on his own shorts, pants, and sweater. He reached into a side pocket of his jeans and pulled out a pack of cigarettes. "*Ça te dérange?*"

Brian shook his head no – it wouldn't bother him. He lifted a small candle from the coffee table and lit Bastien's cigarette. Bastien took a long drag and handed it to Brian. Brian took a puff and handed it back. He reached for his glass of wine and took a long sip.

"So, you are here for the week?" Bastien asked, searching for small talk to ease their eventual parting.

"Yes. My friends arrive tomorrow. You'll have to meet them."

Bastien nodded, but knew it was unlikely to happen. Like Brian, he enjoyed a quick *rendezvous*, but nothing more. He had already explored Brian's profile online and knew Brian wasn't boyfriend material. They had a nice time together, and perhaps they could do another round, but neither wanted more.

"So, who was the guy at the bar today? He seemed uncomfortable."

"He was. Since my car was being repaired at his garage, he drove me here in the storm. He's Muslim. When he found out I was gay – well, you can imagine."

Bastien raised his brows. "Muslim! And he knew you were gay?"

Brian nodded. He looked off into the distance and then said, "But it was curious. The more we talked, the more interested he seemed in hearing my story. I got the feeling he was conflicted."

"Do you think he was gay?"

"Definitely not. But he seemed intrigued, as if my past could illuminate something troubling in his own life."

Bastien raised his brows. "What did he find intriguing?"

"It's complicated, but the short version is that my parents threw me out of the house when I was a teenager. That seemed unimaginable to him."

"How horrible," Bastien noted.

"What, that he was troubled?"

"No, that your parents kicked you out of the house. I can't fathom that."

Brian's eyes watered. Even after so many years, the reality of their rejection was still painful and troubling.

"I'm surprised the Arab was moved. They don't seem too compassionate about those matters."

"That was my initial fear, but as we got to know each other, he seemed more tolerant and thoughtful."

"Be on guard," Bastien warned him.

"I am. But he seemed sincere."

"And you?" Brian interjected, wanting to move the uncomfortable conversation away from himself and toward Bastien. "*Copain?*"

"I'm not really boyfriend material," Bastien began, realizing he and Brian were a lot alike. "I like my freedom and independence."

Brian nodded. "What do you do?"

"Lawyer. With the government."

Brian raised his brow. "That's surprising. I would have taken you for a manager, more entrepreneurial."

"How so?"

"I don't know. It was just something I was picking up."

"Funny. That's what I wanted to be growing up, but my parents pushed me into law."

"Do they live around here?"

"They're in Montreal."

"At least they're close."

"They could be around the corner, and it wouldn't matter."

Brian gave Bastien an inquisitive look.

"My story's not that different from yours. Only it's a bit more sordid. I was molested by an uncle. I accused him, but my father blamed me."

"You're kidding."

"No. I wish I were. My parents came up with all sorts of reasons why I was the problem. My father tried to buy me off with an expensive education and law school. I went along since it was the path of least resistance and, well, I'm doing okay for myself."

"But you're carrying all of that shit with you."

Brian and Bastien both stared at each other, recognizing their own sadness and pain in each other's eyes. It was a deflating end to an otherwise delightful and tantalizing encounter.

Bastien raised his glass and said, "Here's to shit! We carry it well, don't we?"

Brian smiled unconvincingly. Although he imagined many of his tricks were medicating emotional pain with sex, it was the first time a lover had so clearly mirrored his own despondency. Success and sex couldn't mask the betrayal and disdain he felt from his parents and from Eric. He reached for Bastien's cigarette and took a long drag. It was going to be a long and insufferable night.

"Well, that was uplifting!" Brian said sarcastically as he exhaled the cigarette smoke.

Bastien chuckled. "At least we're not tied down in a boring marriage with children. I would die."

"Me, too," Brian said, although he would give anything for a long-term relationship. He just didn't trust love anymore. It seemed unreliable and unattainable.

"Well, I'd better go. It's a school night."

"You don't have to. You can stay if you'd like. We're alone."

Bastien shook his head. Yes, they were alone, and he felt alone, but he didn't want to get involved, to get attached. Better to walk away. "I'd love to, but it's an early morning tomorrow."

"I understand," Brian said, placing his hand affectionately on

Bastien's thigh. He did understand. The best remedy for a broken heart was a hard shell, and they both had perfected theirs.

Bastien rose and gave Brian a long, warm kiss. Brian helped him with his coat, scarf, hat, and gloves. He embraced him and showed him to the door. He returned to the sofa in his shorts and enjoyed the warmth of the fireplace. It had been a long and momentous day, and before long, he dozed off.

4

Chapter Four – Friends

Roberto drove up, and Brian walked out to greet him. Roberto rolled down the window and smiled warmly at Brian. They exchanged kisses on the cheek. "There's a space just up the road I cleared for you. Why don't you park, and I will help you in with your luggage?"

Roberto nodded. He put the car in gear, edged it forward over the compacted surface, and carefully inched the car into a spot dug out of large drifts. He got out of the car and said, "I can't believe how much snow there is." He walked to the back of the car, opened the trunk, and pulled out a large suitcase.

"The skiing will be great!" Brian remarked.

"If we can get there," Roberto said with alarm.

"They're used to it here. We'll be fine."

"I'm eager to see the place," Roberto said, as he walked up the steps onto the porch and through the front door. "Wow! This is nice. We did well."

Brian nodded. "It's very nice. I assume you and I can share the

2nd bath, and David and Carlos can take the room with the en suite bath. Here's your room."

"Nice. This will do," Roberto said as he entered the room and dropped his suitcase near the bed.

"Is that a new sweater?" Brian inquired as Roberto unpacked.

He nodded. "Do you like it?"

Brian rubbed his hands over Roberto's shoulder. "Love the fabric."

"It's Italian."

"Of course it is. It's got a nice cut to it."

Although Brian and Roberto had gone on a few dates many years ago, they realized they could never be lovers. They were both too mercurial for each other. But Brian always found Roberto attractive, breathtakingly so. He was a solid, muscular man with broad shoulders, a large head, dark hair, and playful dark brown eyes. From time to time, he grew a beard but, at the moment, was clean shaven. He had a prominent jaw and a long, sensual nose that Brian found delicious.

"Wine?" Brian offered. "There are also cheese and crackers, if you like."

"I would love a glass of wine. It was a long trip, first to Montreal, then here after a layover. When do David and Carlos arrive?"

"I think in about an hour. We can take a walk and get dinner later."

"Sounds great."

"So, tell me more about this Arab you met."

"He's a north African, a Moroccan. At first, I was nervous. He was religiously conservative and seemed offended by my being gay. There were several tense moments."

"But? I detect a but."

"Well, the conversation became less radical and more dialogical, as if we were trying to make sense of things together. It was very odd – something I never imagined."

"Was he cute?"

"Roberto!"

"Well?"

"In a way, yes. He had dark caramel skin, short dark hair, a trim beard, and dark alluring eyes."

"Those will do it every time."

"But he's older – my father's age. He does have an adorable son."

"You met his son?"

"No. He showed me a photo."

"Can we meet him?"

"Roberto! I don't want to get killed by an angry, religiously conservative father. Let's stick with the cute local Quebecois men!"

"Have you identified any yet?"

"I did some preliminary reconnaissance – and well."

"No! Already?"

Brian nodded, blushing.

"You move quickly."

"We only have a week."

"Can we share?"

Brian glared at him. "Find your own!" Brian said with a humorous edge.

Brian lit a fire, and he and Roberto caught up while they sipped wine. A few hours later, David and Carlos arrived in a taxi. As they walked in, everyone exchanged kisses and hugs. David and Carlos unpacked and joined Brian and Roberto in the parlor for appetizers and drinks.

David was a successful lawyer from Atlanta. He was quiet and cerebral. Carlos added levity and flare to their relationship. He was of Cuban extraction; his grandparents having immigrated during one of the first waves of people to leave the island in the 60s. His playful personality was a hit at the private school where he taught second graders.

"Where should we go for dinner tonight?" Roberto asked.

"There are a couple of nice places at the bottom of the hill – and some in the upper part of the city," Brian noted.

"Any suggestions?" Carlos pressed.

"There was a place I passed yesterday with a lot of cute guys going in and out. Maybe we should try that. I'll see if we can get reservations."

"Sounds great. And tomorrow, skiing?" David asked.

"We have reservations for rental equipment at Mont-Sainte-Anne. It's about thirty minutes from here. The conditions should be incredible with all the fresh snow."

"I can't wait," Roberto exclaimed.

Later that evening, they bundled up and walked down the hill to the lower part of the city, and entered a cozy, upscale restaurant on a side street. It had tall ceilings and large black and white prints decorating old brick walls. The lighting was dim and colorful, adding a certain ethereal feel to the space.

Heads turned as they walked through the door and approached the maître d'. Roberto's gaze darted back and forth, surveying the crowd. David and Carlos were focused on getting a good table, and Brian exchanged a few glances with a handsome guy at the bar who stared his way.

They were seated, and Carlos said, "Brian, great recommendation. What a crowd."

"Hm," Brian sighed, continuing to gaze toward the bar.

They ordered drinks and first courses. Half-way into the first course, Roberto said in a low voice, "*Cazzo* – what the fuck!"

David, Carlos, and Brian all looked up from their plates.

"It's Eric."

"My Eric?" Brian asked, alarmed.

Roberto nodded. He glanced across the room. Brian followed his gaze and noticed Eric seated with another man, holding hands, and sipping Champagne.

"I think I'm going to get sick," Brian noted. "Of all the places. I never see him in Boston or Ptown, but here he is."

"Go say something to him," David prodded.

"No. I'm not desperate."

"It would show *cojones*," Carlos noted. "Let him know you're not intimidated.

"I'll show you *cojones*," Brian continued. He stood up and walked toward the bar and approached the guy who had been cruising him earlier. "*Ciao, Je suis Brian.*"

"*Betrand. Enchanté.*"

"*Vous parlez anglais?*"

"*Un petit peu. Et toi, français?*"

"*Assez* – enough."

"A drink?" Bertrand offered.

Brian nodded. "Just a quick one. Then I have to get back to my friends."

Bertrand waved down the bartender and looked inquisitively at Brian, who said, "*Un verre de vin rouge, merci.*"

Bertrand and Brian visited. Brian positioned himself where Eric eventually noticed him. They both evaded making eye contact, but Brian had achieved his goal. Brian excused himself, gave his number to Bertrand, and rejoined Roberto, David, and Carlos.

"That was smooth!" Carlos said.

"We took the liberty of ordering you a steak - rare. Looks like that will be the menu this evening," Roberto said playfully.

Brian took a long sip of his wine. He leaned over to Roberto and asked, "You don't mind if I take a detour on the way home this evening, do you?"

Roberto looked disappointed, but not surprised at Brian's facility for picking up guys. "Go for it!"

Their meals came, and they began to eat in earnest, all famished from their journeys.

"I love the artistic presentation of the food," Carlos noted, cutting a juicy piece of filet and, afterwards, piercing thin shafts of asparagus that were laying on a creamy bed of risotto.

"Hm," David murmured as he chewed on a piece of the meat. "And the herb butter is amazing."

Brian nodded, still glancing at Bertrand from time to time, and taking in the rest of the room. Aside from Eric and his dinner guest, they were the only Americans in the place. Although most were presumably bilingual, everyone was speaking French. Brian listened in, savoring its distinctive cadence and sounds. The four guys nearest them were enthusiastic about a play that had just opened. One of their companions was the lead actor. The other table seemed engrossed in gossip about a couple who had just split up. Ironically, one of them looked over at Brian and winked.

Roberto said in observation, "I love how people dress up here. In the winter, people in the States all look like they've been on a hike in the woods – thick old boots, dingy jeans, bulky sweaters, and no makeup."

"Dear, you just spend too much time in Cambridge when you visit Boston. You need to come to the Seaport or the South End. We know how to dress there!" Brian remarked.

"I've been to the Seaport. Too many rich corporate urban postgrads," Roberto retorted.

"At least they're cute!" Brian countered.

"And expensive."

"Hon, I never pay," Brian noted, cocking his head back.

"Neither do we," Carlos said, smiling warmly into David's face.

Brian felt a sharp pang race through his chest at Carlos's remark. He was proud of his independence, but often wondered if he shouldn't settle down. He cut another piece of steak and, as he put it in his mouth, he glanced over at Carlos and David and then at Bertrand sitting at the bar. For the moment, the intrigue and thrill of the chase was preferable to coupledom.

They finished their meals and, as they were waiting for coffee, Eric and his boyfriend stood up and walked through the room. Eric caught Brian's eye and said with fake affect, "Brian. What a surprise."

Brian stood up and gave Eric a cold embrace. "Eric, you know Roberto. And this is David and Carlos."

"Nice to meet you," he replied. "And this is Peter."

They all nodded.

"You here for Winter Carnival?" Eric asked.

"Yes. And a bit of skiing."

Eric seemed eager to leave and said, "Well. It was nice to see you. Let's catch up sometime. Enjoy your stay."

Brian air kissed him and extended his hand to Peter. They left. Brian excused himself, took his espresso to the bar, and joined Bertrand, who was finishing his meal.

"Who was that? Even I could detect fangs from here," Bertrand asked.

"My ex. I haven't seen him in for some time. What are the chances?"

"And your friends?"

"They're heading home. And you?"

"Me too. You want to come over for a drink?"

"Would love to."

Roberto, David, and Carlos waved to Brian as he and Bertrand began to put on their coats at the door. "I live nearby," Bertrand remarked.

Two hours later, Brian returned home. Roberto was sitting in front of the fireplace, reading a book.

"So, how was he?"

Brian didn't reply at first. He took off his coat and unlaced his boots. "Let me go get a glass of wine. I'll be right back."

"Can you pour me one, too?"

Brian nodded as went into the kitchen. He opened a bottle of red and poured two generous glasses. He returned and sat down next to Roberto.

"Well?"

Again, Brian didn't reply right away. He was deep in thought.

"What's wrong? Did he have a small one? Was he too rough with you?"

"No. He was well-endowed, handsome, tender, and perfect in all ways."

"And?"

"I couldn't come."

"You? That's not possible. Don't you usually come multiple times with a trick?"

"I know. I'm a legend," he said jokingly. "Something was off."

"I'm sorry, *mon chéri*. You must be stressed at work or something. It can happen to anyone."

"No. Things at work are good, and I'm relaxed here."

"How did he react?"

"He was the perfect gentleman. He kept trying to help me along. He said not to worry – that I was handsome and adorable."

"That killer smile."

"Hm, hum," Brian murmured as he drifted off in his mind.

"Well, I'm sure it's only temporary – perhaps the cold, too much wine, or something like that."

"And you, did you hook up with anyone?"

"There was a cutie that popped up on my feed, but when I reached out, he was already busy. I decided to stay home and read."

Brian stared at him.

"I know. It's not like me."

"What's happening to us?" Brian lamented.

"We're getting old, *papi!*"

"Don't call me that. You know I hate it!"

"Okay. But you must admit, we don't have the stamina and energy we had before. Maybe we need to settle down."

"You mean a long-term? A boyfriend? A husband?" Brian asked nervously.

"Yeah. Maybe It's time."

"I don't know. Seeing Eric tonight reminded me of why I have no intention of settling down. It was too painful."

"Maybe that's it."

"What?"

"Maybe seeing Eric did something to you psychologically. Maybe that's why." Roberto said without elaboration.

"I don't think that has anything to do with it. On the contrary, it should have excited me to prove that I'm over him, that I can have fun when I want without strings attached."

"Maybe that's what you were doing – trying to prove something. That's never a good thing in sex," Roberto suggested.

"I didn't mean I was trying to prove something. It's just that I have the ideal life – a great job, friends, and lots of sex."

"What about love?" Roberto asked.

"What about it?"

"Don't you want love?"

The question unnerved Brian. Estranged from his parents and betrayed by his ex, love was not something he felt he could wish for. He hated that Roberto had put his finger on the issue. He was defiant in maintaining he didn't need love. He had his friends. They were his family. They were the emotional support and companionship he needed, treasured, and enjoyed.

Brian didn't respond. He took another long sip of wine and stared at Roberto. "And you? Why don't you settle down?"

"The right one hasn't come along, but I'm ready."

"Well, I'm not. I like my freedom. What's better than a fun week away with best friends, snow, great food, and cute boys?"

"What happens when we get to the point where we have to pay for cute boys?"

"We'll deal with that when we reach that point. It's a long way off."

"You think so, dear?"

Brian nodded. He stood up, poked a long iron into the hot embers and spread them inside the stone fireplace so they would die down. "I'm ready for bed. Do you mind if I use the bathroom first?"

"I'll be in soon."

"*Bonne nuit.*

"*Bonne nuit, chéri.*"

5

Chapter Five – Omar

Two days later, Brian's phone pinged with a text from Hakim: "Brian. Your car is ready. My nephew, Omar, is a student at Laval University. He is going to drive the car up this morning and leave it with you. If you are at the apartment, he can give you the keys. If not, he will park it on the street and leave the keys in a secure place."

Brian texted back: "Hakim. Thanks. That's great news. I have some work to do, so I'll stay at the apartment and wait for him. Will you send me an invoice?"

Hakim: "Yes. We will send it to your email address. We have your credit card on file."

Brian walked toward the kitchen where Carlos, David, and Roberto were having breakfast. "Hey guys, the garage is going to bring my car to me this morning. I think I'll stay here and do some work. Why don't you go ski on your own?"

"We can wait for you," Roberto offered, disappointed to miss a day of skiing with Brian.

"That's okay. I have some work I have to take care of. We'll ski tomorrow."

"Why don't you come join us later, after the car arrives?" David suggested.

"Sounds good. I'll text you when I'm on my way."

Brian went into his room and opened his laptop. Roberto, David, and Carlos dressed for the cold winter day and headed out.

Around 11:00, the doorbell rang. Brian went to the door and pulled it open. He gasped for air and felt his heart pound rapidly as he glanced at the handsome man standing on the porch.

"*Je m'appelle Omar. J'ai votre voiture.*"

"*Enchanté. Je m'appelle Brian.* Come in."

Omar paused at the door, staring at Brian, who had a difficult time extracting himself from Omar's deep, dark eyes. They were large orbs encircled by thick lashes and brows that narrowed in deep creases near his temple, giving him a weepy teddy bear look. As Omar unwrapped his scarf and took off his hat, he broke into a soft, gentle smile. His caramel skin quickly lost its redness from the cold outside, and his dark wavy hair glistened in the overhead light.

"Let me take your coat," Brian offered.

"I don't want to take your time," Omar said apologetically.

"Don't be silly," Brian responded. "The least I can do is offer you something warm to drink. It's so cold outside."

Omar nodded, looking around the room. "Nice place you have."

"It's just a rental. I'm here with friends for Winter Carnival."

"My uncle said you had an accident on your way here from Boston. I think you two spent some time together during the storm."

"Yes. It was quite the adventure. I thought I was going to have two accidents in one day."

Omar chuckled.

"Some tea or coffee or hot chocolate?"

"I'll have some coffee if it isn't too much trouble," Omar said, continuing to observe the surroundings.

"Espresso or American?"

"American, if you have it."

Brian nodded and retreated to the kitchen. As he began to prepare the coffee, he murmured to himself, trying to contain his excitement, "Oh my God. He's gorgeous. Drop dead gorgeous. Get hold of yourself."

He spooned some coffee into a filter, filled the container with water, and turned on the maker. He walked back out into the living room and said, "Have a seat. It will be ready in a minute."

Omar took a seat in one of the large stuffed chairs facing the fireplace, where a few dying embers continued to glow orange. He looked nervous.

Brian put a couple of fresh logs on the fire and asked, "So, your uncle said you are a student at Laval?"

Omar nodded, rubbing his hands anxiously over his thighs.

"What do you study?"

"Theoretical physics."

Brian raised his brows and said, "Wow, that's impressive!" He had expected business or finance or mechanics, but not theoretical physics. He imagined, as part of a close-knit immigrant family, Omar would have been expected to continue the family business. "What do you plan to do with theoretical physics – it's not a particularly practical field of study?"

"I'm hoping to teach or do research. I'm finishing my doctoral studies."

Brian raised his brows again.

"And you, what do you do?" Omar asked.

"I'm in biomedical research."

Now it was time for Omar to be surprised. He had noticed

Brian's light turquoise nails, his slim frame, his stylish haircut, and his exaggerated gestures. He imagined Brian was a designer, artist, architect, or perhaps someone in retail. He, in turn, raised his brows and smiled.

Brian excused himself, went into the kitchen, jumped up and down excitedly in place, took a deep breath, poured two cups of coffee, and returned to the living room.

"*Voilà! Crème, sucre?*

"No. I take it black," Omar replied, taking a sip from the steaming cup. "Biomedical research is a big business in Boston. Did you study there, too?"

"Hm, hum," Brian replied, evading the disclosure of his pedigree MIT and Harvard credentials, although Omar's studies at Laval were equally impressive. "By the way, do you work with your uncles?"

"I used to until I went to school. I still help from time to time. As you can imagine, it's a close-knit family business."

"Were you born here?"

Omar nodded. "I was born here several years after my parents immigrated."

"Have you been to Morocco?"

"Once, as a child. And you, are you from Boston?"

"Atlanta."

"Parents? Siblings?"

"Painful story. Yes, and no. I have parents, but we don't see each other."

"I'm sorry. I can't imagine."

Brian nodded.

Both stared at each other, searching for a topic to sustain their conversation. Neither wanted their chat to end, but neither knew where to take it. Omar started. "So, you are here skiing?" he asked, glancing toward the skis propped against the door.

"Yes. With friends. They are at Mont-Sainte-Anne today."

"I've always wanted to ski. It's odd with all this time in Quebec, I've never gone."

"I don't imagine your parents grew up skiing," Brian said with a chuckle.

"No. They hate the cold, although they have gotten used to it."

"Do you have siblings?"

"A sister – and a lot of cousins."

"Do any of them ski?"

"I have a few that do. My parents were always frugal, saving money for our education. So, we didn't indulge."

"Do you live on campus?"

"I have a small apartment off-campus."

"Work?"

"I help my uncles, and I have a teaching assistant position at the university."

"You must keep busy."

Omar nodded. They continued to visit – discussing family backgrounds, sites in Quebec, and science. Eventually, Omar said, "Well, thanks for the coffee. I need to get back to the university."

"I'll take you," Brian offered eagerly.

"No. I was planning to take the bus. It's an easy ride from the center of the town."

"Don't be silly, as we say in English. I'll take you. It's the least I can do."

Omar turned red. Brian assumed it was Omar's shy way of agreeing and perhaps an involuntary bodily response to his interest in Brian. At least Brian hoped that was the case. His gaydar was off. He found French Canadian men difficult to read, and he had little experience with North Africans. Omar was handsome and attractive, but he seemed straight acting and serious. He glanced at his hand and noticed it was ringless.

"Let me get my coat and gloves. I'll be right with you."

Brian retreated to his room, brushed his teeth, and returned with coat, hat, and gloves in hand. He put them on, wrapped a scarf around his neck, and opened the door for Omar, who had put his coat on earlier. They walked out into the bright sunlight that only barely taken a dent out of the bitterly cold air.

Brian took a walk around the right front side of the gray Volvo and said, "Amazing. You can't even tell that the car smashed into the tree. Your uncles did a great job."

"They are good. That's why their business is successful."

"Let's go," Brian said as he opened the driver's door and took a seat. He cranked on the engine, turned on the seat warmers, and proceeded carefully over the snow-packed road. "What direction?" he asked Omar.

Omar pointed toward a small side street that led to Rue-Saint-Jean and then eventually to a larger boulevard that headed west toward the university.

Omar continued to give instructions. He kept his head facing forward, but he twisted his eyes sideways to observe Brian undetected. Omar had always been attracted to men. He had a crush on one of his uncles as a boy, obsessed over a teammate in high school, and cruised men on campus. His sexual experiences had been few – a distant cousin visiting from Morocco who shared his bed during a family vacation, a troubled brief relationship during his freshman year in college, and a few disappointing hook ups on dating apps.

His friends and family all presumed he was straight, and there was intense pressure from his extended family for him to marry and start a family. When home from college, he had little opportunity to socialize outside the local immigrant community. He reluctantly went on a few first and second dates with women his family pushed his way. He was, in theory, moving toward a marriage proposal with a distant cousin. As a Muslim, he was marginalized at the university. He was cruised, from time to time, but never felt confident enough to pursue opportunities and always worried that if a relationship started, news would get back to his parents.

His fascination and attraction to Brian was surprising. Brian was fair, thin, and flamboyant. Omar was usually drawn to darker, more masculine types. Brian had an affable smile and a warm, gentle demeanor that made Omar feel at ease. The fact that he was a biomedical research scientist was baffling and intriguing. He wanted to learn more.

"Here. Just up the way. That's my building – à droite. Merci beaucoup."

During the short drive to Omar's apartment, Brian had been rehearsing a pretext for keeping their conversation going. His palms began to sweat, and he felt his pulse race as he feared he might have to say goodbye. Tentatively, he said, "I was going to grab some lunch. Do you know any good places around here?"

Omar sighed, relieved at an opening. "Actually, I was going to get some lunch, too. There's a great pizza place just around the corner. Would you like to get something together?"

Brian nodded.

"Why don't you park here?" Omar said, pointing to a space. "It's a short walk."

Brian parked, paid the meter, and locked the car as they walked down the sidewalk and around the corner. Piles of snow lined the pavement, and there was a stiff wind blowing between several mid-sized apartment buildings. An épicerie, liquor store, cleaner, and Italian restaurant lined a section of the side street. Omar said, "This is the pizza place – or perhaps I should say – an Italian restaurant. I hope you'll like it."

Brian smiled as they entered. Food was not on his mind.

The server showed them a table along a brick-faced wall covered in large photographs of Italian monuments. She dropped a couple of menus on the table and asked if they wanted something to drink.

"*Un verre du vin rouge, s'il vous plaît,*" Brian began.

"*Moi aussi,*" Omar followed.

"You drink wine?" Brian asked, raising his brow.

"Ah, yes. You probably had dinner with my uncle. My family is very observant and devout – no wine, only *halal* meat, fasting during Ramadan, prayers facing Mecca."

"And you're not?" Brian asked.

"Well, when I'm home, I am. When I'm here at school, not so much."

"Do you not believe?"

Omar wrung his hands nervously, formulating a response. Religion wasn't what he wanted to talk about, but as a Muslim, it inevitably became a focus with new acquaintances. He was both embarrassed and proud to be a Muslim – a gnawing ambivalence about his identity.

"It's complicated. I believe in God – or Allah, as we say. I love my family, and I respect their traditions, traditions that are at some level comforting. But, as a scientist, I'm torn. I feel like we are on the cusp of a new way of thinking about God, religion, and spirituality."

Brian smiled and nodded.

"And you?" Omar asked.

"Am I a Muslim?" Brian said jokingly. "Do I look Muslim?"

"We're not all North African or Middle Eastern, you know."

"Point made!" Brian said.

The server came with their glasses of red wine. They lifted their glasses and, in unison, said, "Cheers."

"I'm not religious. I was raised Catholic, but no longer find it compelling."

"For scientific reasons?" Omar suggested.

"No, more for personal ones."

Brian felt an intense chemistry with Omar and sensed it was reciprocal, but Omar didn't seem gay, and he feared if he broached the subject, the magic of the moment might be lost. He needed a few more confirming signs.

"Ah," Omar said, not pressing Brian to continue.

"So, what will you do once you finish your studies? I don't imagine Sherbrooke has jobs for physicists."

Omar chucked and smiled. "No, it doesn't. I wouldn't mind staying here in Quebec City. Or perhaps Montreal. I've even considered Boston, given the profile of the universities there."

As Omar mentioned Boston, Brian's heart pounded. He wondered why he was reacting so spontaneously to Omar.

"I suppose it would be nice to start a family near your extended family," Brian offered, hoping Omar might disavow such a scenario.

Omar glanced evasively off into the distance. Brian was more intrigued by the possibility that Omar might not be as straight as he seemed. Omar said, "Hm, yes and no. It can be a bit confining. I'm not in a hurry."

"Haven't found the right lady yet?" Brian asked pointedly.

Omar decided he had nothing to lose. He said calmly, "Or the right man."

Brian grinned. "Well, well, well."

Omar blushed. The server approached their table. "*Pour manger?*"

"*Qu'est-ce que tu veux? Une pizza? Une margherita avec champignons?*" Omar asked.

"*Oui,*" Brian agreed quickly to the mushroom pizza, ready to get rid of the server and continue the interrogation.

"So, where were we? Not the right man yet. Right?"

Omar blushed again and tried to conceal a smile as he took a sip of wine.

Brian continued, "That must be challenging, given what Hakim said to me the other day."

Omar looked worried. "What did he say?" He hesitated and haltingly inquired, "And you?"

Brian nodded. "Yes. Well, it's hard to conceal. It came up in conversation. Your uncle is very inquisitive and confrontational."

"Yes. I think that's his way of protecting the family."

"He said God is compassionate, and I said I didn't need compassion. I need love. He wasn't happy with me."

"Yes, I can imagine!"

"He didn't say anything about me to you?" Brian pressed, wondering if Omar had been warned.

"No. In fact, it was a little curious that he asked me to bring the car to you. Another uncle had an appointment in Lévis, and Hakim could have picked him up on the way back from Saint-Marie."

"Hm," Brian murmured, wondering if Hakim might be more open-minded than he let on and more aware of Omar's dilemma.

"Do you think Hakim knows about you?"

Omar shook his head emphatically. "No one knows. I go on dates with women and talk about marriage. I can't imagine anyone suspects."

Brian wasn't convinced, or at least it wouldn't have surprised him if Hakim was on to his nephew.

"So, you're not out."

"No. It's impossible. I would be disowned or, worse, beaten to a pulp. That's why I'm thinking about moving to another city."

"That's horrible."

Omar nodded. "And you? You mentioned your family. Is it a problem?"

Brian nodded, his eyes watering.

"I'm sorry."

"No. It's okay. I don't get to talk about it much. Yes. It's a problem. My parents are conservative Catholics who threw me out of the house when I was 17. I haven't seen them since."

This was precisely what Omar feared, and Brian could see the horror written all over his face.

"And yet you are a successful researcher. How did you manage that?"

"I was fortunate to have been taken in by a loving and supportive family. I got scholarships and applied myself. I was determined to show them that there was nothing wrong with me."

Omar nodded; sensing Brian's story was his as well.

Their pizza arrived. They raised their glasses again, took sips of wine, and began to cut into the pizza. Omar observed Brian as he gracefully cut pieces of pizza and placed them artfully in his mouth. There was an elegance to his movements and a sophistication that tempered his otherwise gender, non-conforming demeanor. Brian wove together an intelligent and thoughtful presence with a boyish and playful energy that was captivating. Omar was already smitten.

Typically, Brian would have been intimidated by someone like Omar — fiercely masculine, handsome, and smart. Omar reminded him of Eric, and that bothered him. But Brian detected a vulnerability in Omar that was endearing. He imagined Omar was sensitive and compassionate – at least he hoped he was.

Brian's phone pinged. Roberto had sent a text: "Brian. Where are you? Are you coming to ski?"

"Sorry," Brian said to Omar. "I have to respond."

He texted back: "Got tied up with work. See you all later for dinner."

Roberto texted back: "Ok. *Ciao.*"

"Do you have to attend to something?" Omar inquired.

"No. It was my friends. I was supposed to join them on the slopes."

"Sorry to have kept you."

"I'm not sorry. What a delightful surprise."

Omar smiled. "*Moi aussi.*"

"Hey! How would you like to go skiing tomorrow? I'd be happy to take you – give you a few lessons."

Omar contemplated Brian's offer, raised his brows, and said, "I just have a few student appointments tomorrow, but I can reschedule them. I can do my research this afternoon. Why not?"

Brian grinned. "Why don't I come pick you up around 8. We'll drive to the mountain and meet my friends."

Omar looked nervous.

"They're harmless."

Omar remained nervous.

"What's the matter?"

"Nothing," he said unconvincingly.

Brian realized Omar probably hadn't hung out with gay people much, and he was probably nervous both about being outed inadvertently or about not fitting in.

"It will be fun. You live in Quebec. You should learn to ski."

"I don't have any ski clothes," Omar protested.

Brian looked straight at the back of Omar's chair and said, "I see you have a ski jacket, and I'm sure you have long underwear and wool socks. Do you have any winter hiking or snow mobile pants?"

Omar shook his head and then said, "There's a guy down the hall who skis. Let me ask him."

"I'll take care of the rest — getting you skis, boots, and helmet."

They finished their lunch, continued to visit, and then Omar said, "If I'm going to join you tomorrow, I better get some work done."

They paid their tab, walked to Brian's car, and embraced. "*Merci beaucoup!*" Brian said warmly.

"Thank you for a surprising afternoon," Omar added.

Brian got into his car, turned on the motor, and rolled down the window, and winked at Omar. Omar waved back as Brian slowly drove away.

6

⚜

Chapter Six –
Learning to Ski

Roberto, Carlos, and David stood shivering in front of the ski rental shop at the base of Mont-Sainte-Anne. The sun was out, but the temperature was hovering in the single digits Fahrenheit. Roberto had insisted they meet Brian and Omar as early as possible. David had never been convinced that Roberto's and Brian's relationship was just friendship. He wondered if Roberto wasn't feeling jealous of Omar. Sure, Brian was always tricking with the locals on his app, but they were never more than a onetime thing, and he and Roberto were inseparable otherwise.

Brian and Omar approached. David extended his hand. "You must be Omar. Nice to meet you. And this is Carlos," he added, holding Carlos tightly next to him.

Omar extended his hand, but his eyes wandered toward Roberto. "Omar," Brian began, "this is Roberto. My best friend. But be careful, he bites!"

Roberto glared at Brian and said, "Dear, I'm surprised by your tone. Did you not have your coffee this morning?" He then turned to Omar. Omar had extended his hand, but Roberto grabbed his shoulders and gave him a kiss on both cheeks. "We're in Quebec. We kiss here!"

Omar grinned and blushed.

"Let's go in and get you fitted for the day," Brian directed while staring down Roberto.

They all entered the shop, which was, thankfully, uncrowded. An efficient team of staff helped Omar find the right size boots, skis, poles, and helmet. He had a dark blue ski jacket, black ski pants he borrowed from a neighbor, and a black pullover sweater under the jacket. The blue jacket made his dark eyes more alluring, and the black sweater made him look sophisticated, even a bit exotic and enigmatic. Brian continued to swoon over him, making sure the boots were properly adjusted and that he had everything he needed for a comfortable day on the slopes. He walked to a nearby desk and purchased a ski pass for him.

They walked outside. There was little wind, so the sun reflecting off the bright snow was warming the air. They carried their skis out onto a large, flat area just at the base of the slopes. Brian looked up and said, "Wow. It's beautiful today."

Carlos nodded and said, "Should we take the gondola up? It might be an easier way to get Omar on the snow without the challenge of getting on and off the chairlift."

"Good idea," Brian said, waving Omar and the rest toward the gondola.

They got in a line that snaked through a large steel shed where gondola cars arrived, slowed, loaded, and then returned to the summit. Omar was mouth agape at the alpine setting – the slopes, the snow-laden fir trees, and beautifully dressed people ready for a day on the mountain. They stepped inside a cabin, the doors closed, the mechanism gripped the cable, and they began the steep ascent.

"So, this is your first day skiing?" David asked thoughtfully.

Omar nodded.

From the side, Roberto grinned, eager to watch the day unfold. He asked, "Omar, how is it you live in Quebec and haven't skied?"

"Well, it's not exactly part of my family's heritage coming from North Africa."

"Ah, yes," Roberto nodded. "Are you excited?"

Omar looked at Brian and nodded. Their glance startled Roberto, who was increasingly convinced something serious was unfolding between them.

At the top of the gondola, they grabbed their skis and walked out onto the snowy surface, where skiers were stepping into bindings, adjusting goggles, and pushing off down the slopes.

Omar looked to Brian for direction.

Brian took Omar's skis and laid them on the snow. "You step into them this way," he said as he stepped into his own ski bindings. Omar imitated him, almost losing his balance at one point. Brian quickly caught him, holding onto Omar's arm as long as he could without it being too obvious they were flirting. Roberto noticed and seemed annoyed, even a bit alarmed.

"Use your poles to balance yourself. Let's walk a little." Brian led Omar around, side stepping up and down the incline and moving slowly forward with small sliding steps. He showed him how to form a snowplow and directed him to point his skis down the gentle incline and then wedge them to slow and stop.

Omar was surprisingly coordinated, getting the hang of things quickly. Carlos, David, and Roberto pushed off and promised to meet Brian and Omar at the bottom of the mountain.

Omar was eager to impress Brian, who, in his dark jacket, red ski pants, and black ski boots, cut quite a figure on the slopes. The day before, he would not have imagined Brian to be the athletic type, much less a downhill skier.

Omar observed the people around him. He felt out of his element – a winter playground filled with white francophones. There were only a few people of color, and certainly no Arabs or North Africans. He was grateful for the helmet and goggles that concealed his ethnicity.

Brian suggested they ski toward a grove of trees about 100 meters below them. "Let your skis go parallel and build up a little speed. When you want to slow, simply form a wedge and press your weight through your boots onto the edges of the skis."

Omar did as instructed, picked up some gentle speed, and found it was relatively easy to stop.

"Now you're ready for turns. When you want to turn left, put more weight on the right wedged ski and turn your body to the left."

Omar pushed off, wedged his skis, and then made a tentative turn. "Bravo!" Brian said excitedly.

Omar smiled proudly.

"Follow me," Brian said, pushing off and making wide, gentle turns back and forth.

Omar had little difficulty picking up the feel and rhythm of the moves quickly.

"Are you ready for some parallel turns?"

"What are they?"

"Watch!" Brian said. He pushed off and made a series of turns where, instead of a wedge, the skis were parallel with each other. He stopped not far below them and said, "Do the same thing you did with the snowplows, but as you make the turn, bring your inside ski in close to the outside ski. It's as if you unweight it and, when you place it near the outside ski, you can put your weight on it again."

Omar let his skis run parallel, picked up some speed, began the snowplow, and then tried to unweight the inside ski and bring it to the outer one. As he did so, he got off balance and fell, landing face forward on the snow. Brian kicked off his skis and ran toward him. "Are you okay?" he asked.

"My pride is wounded, but I'm fine. *Pas de problème.*"

"I would be surprised if you didn't fall. It's part of the initiation process."

"*Mais regarde ce petit garçon*," Omar pointed out a four-year-old racing past them.

"They have a low center of gravity. You're a grown man. It takes more coordination, and the stakes are riskier because there's more distance to the ground!"

Brian reached his hand to Omar, who took hold. Brian lifted him up and dusted snow off his coat. He gazed into his eyes, a protracted and charged look. He wanted to kiss him but held back. He wondered if Omar felt the same.

Each time Omar looked to Brian, who was patiently and playfully coaching him, he felt his legs go weak and his heart race. He wanted to impress him, to gain his esteem, and ultimately to see if there might be something more.

Omar tried a few more turns and gradually gained a sense of balance as he carved turns, weighting and unweighting his skis.

"I've never seen an adult learn so quickly," Brian remarked, proud of him.

"I'm sweating like a pig!" Omar said, breathing heavy after a series of turns but delighted that Brian thought he was doing well.

"Eventually, it will become easier, and you will be relaxed and cool as a cucumber."

They made their way to the bottom of the mountain and to the gondola station. Carlos, David, and Roberto skied up behind them, having made an extra run while Brian and Omar had made their way more slowly.

"How's it going?" David inquired.

"Good," Brian said. "Omar seems to be a natural."

Roberto looked up. He was removing his gloves and had been flirting with a skier who skidded up behind him. He was distracted. There were a lot of handsome guys taking a break after their runs. Roberto had always been a head turner, and he was getting a lot of attention. But he was jealous of Omar, and despite several handsome opportunities looking his way, he stood close to Brian.

"Shall we?" Brian asked, looking at the entrance to the gondola, suggesting another ride to the top.

Everyone nodded.

During the ascent, Roberto said, "Did you see that group of guys a few cabins ahead of us? Delicious!"

"Take it easy, sparky. You just arrived," David said.

"I know, but I lost a couple of days because of the storm."

"I'm sure you'll make up for lost time," Carlos remarked, poking Roberto with one if his ski poles.

Omar glanced at Brian, who, sensing Omar's discomfort, quickly changed subjects. "Roberto, does your research team do any work here in Canada? Isn't Quebec City becoming a biotech center?"

Roberto nodded and mumbled a barely perceptible, "Hm, hum." He glanced out the window, as if uninterested in the topic.

Brian noticed Omar was picking up on Roberto's indifference as his right leg began to shake nervously. He tried another subject. "I'm still amazed at how extensive this mountain is. Should we try the slopes on the north side?"

David and Carlos nodded. Roberto didn't respond. Brian was now officially perturbed. "Roberto, what do you suggest we do next?"

"Well, I'd love to ski La Crete, on the far side. It's got some great sections with steep inclines," Roberto said, with a hint of resentment that Omar was limiting their options.

"It must be expert terrain?" Brian asked, already knowing the answer.

Roberto nodded and grinned, glancing furtively at Omar.

"Any intermediate detours along the way?" Brian inquired.

"Not that I'm aware of."

Omar interjected, "I don't want to hold you guys up. I have enough basics to practice for a while. Why don't you guys do some of the more difficult runs, and I can meet you at the bottom of the mountain later?"

Roberto looked inquisitively at Brian, who was staring at Omar, trying to take a read.

"Why don't I ski with Omar, and you and David and Carlos can ski the blacks?"

"No. I insist," Omar said emphatically. "I'm good for a while. I need to practice the basics. Why don't we meet up in an hour? You can critique me then," Omar said to Brian.

The gondola arrived at the terminus, and they exited the cabin. They walked out onto the snowy surface, plopped their skis on the snow, stepped into the bindings, and adjusted gloves, helmets, and goggles.

"Are you sure you're okay, Omar?" Brian asked again.

"I'll meet you in an hour. Why don't we meet over there?" he suggested, pointing to a restaurant with great panoramic views.

Brian nodded. "*À bientôt.*"

"*Ciao,*" Omar replied.

Carlos, David, Roberto, and Brian pushed off toward the expert slopes, and Omar descended carefully and slowly down the beginner slope.

Brian was unsettled about having left Omar on his own. He was annoyed with Roberto, who was being a prick. He pushed past Roberto and skied aggressively down the mountain, carving

tight turns in the fresh powder. He unleashed his agitation onto
the surface of the snow. As he reached the bottom of the series of
challenging sections of the mountain, he skidded to a stop and took
several deep breaths. He savored the moment of solitude from his
friends, taking in the breathtaking snow, sunshine, and surrounding
forest. He longed to be with Omar, and that unnerved him. He
was there to ski with his friends, but his thoughts were elsewhere.
Carlos, David, and Roberto arrived a few minutes later, all three
being excellent skiers, but not as confident or fast as Brian.

"Wow, Brian! You were flying!" Roberto noted.

"The snow is forgiving. It's not too often one gets these conditions in the East," he replied, concealing the actual reasons for his
aggressive run.

"Still. You were smoking!"

"You all think Omar's okay?" Brian inquired pensively.

"I'm sure he is, but if you want to ski with him, we're fine doing
our own thing, aren't we, Roberto?" David said pointedly.

"This was supposed to be our opportunity to ski together. If I
had known we were going to be teaching a beginner, I would have
rethought things," Roberto said harshly.

"Well, sweetie, if you had found a hottie on the bunny slopes,
you'd be singing a different tune," Brian said bitingly.

"So, Omar's a hottie. Hm, maybe if you're into Middle Eastern
types."

"It's not about whether Omar is a hottie or not. I invited him.
He's nice. It's good to make new friends, particularly in foreign
countries."

"I prefer the local francophones," Roberto said, cocking his head
backward.

Carlos noted, "Omar is a francophone, dear."

"That's not his *Muttersprache*," Roberto replied in German, showing off.

"It actually is his mother tongue, you pretentious queen," Carlos noted with biting humor, poking a ski pole at him.

"There's nothing pretentious about this," Roberto said, waving his hand as if gesturing to the masses.

Carlos and David chuckled. Brian glared at him.

"Let's take this lift up again. I agreed to meet Omar at the restaurant on top. Maybe we can get another run in before then."

They rode to the top, made a quick descent, and rode the gondola up once more. Carlos, David, and Roberto skied off on the north side, and Brian kicked off his skies and stood in the sun, waiting for Omar.

He glanced up the hill and noticed a large person making careful turns back and forth and realized it was Omar. He was in full control and making graceful turns back and forth. Omar looked toward the lodge, and Brian waved. Omar skied up to him and made a careful stop.

"Wow! Impressive. It looks like you have the hang of it," Brian noted.

Omar took off his helmet. He was perspiring. He beamed and his dark hair rustled in the wind. His deep-set eyes were open wide, filled with excitement. "So, you saw that?"

"Yes. You're doing great. Do you want to go inside to get something to eat or drink?"

Omar nodded. "First, I have to pee."

He kicked off his skies, braced them against a rack, and hurried toward the lodge. Brian followed him. Later, they asked for a table at the restaurant.

"Aren't the others coming?"

"They might. We don't need to wait for them."

"I feel bad coming between you and your friends."

"That's their problem – or, I should say, Roberto's problem. There have been plenty of other times when people joined our little gaggle. It's ordinarily a welcoming group."

"What's wrong, then?"

"Nothing," Brian said. The server approached and took their drink orders.

"Roberto seems annoyed."

Brian shook his head but realized Omar might be right.

"It's just the delay in getting the vacation started. He'll be fine once he gets some skiing in – and perhaps finds a cute French man."

Omar asked himself if he might not be Brian's conquest, if Brian had been on the prowl and he was first pickings. It didn't seem that way – but he wondered. Their meeting had been so unusual and unlikely, and he sensed they both felt the instant chemistry. All that mattered now was that he was seated across from an affable, charming, and intelligent man who was classy and cute at the same time.

Brian got a text from Carlos: "We found a place to get a drink and burger on the other side. Why don't we meet you guys later?"

"In an hour at the top of the gondola?"

"Perfect," Carlos answered.

A server came, took their orders, and returned promptly with two beers. They lifted their glasses and Brian said, "To a new ski prodigy!"

"To winter in Quebec!"

"It changes the perspective on things to get outdoors and enjoy the snow."

Omar nodded.

"So, do you think you would do this again, or is it a one-shot deal?" Brian asked with a bit of double entendre.

The opening wasn't wasted on Omar, who replied, "I hope there's more!"

Brian blushed, hiding his face behind the glass of beer.

They continued to visit, eat, people watch, and then bundled up for the cold and walked out to meet Carlos, David, and Roberto, who were standing by a clump of trees adjusting equipment. They waved as Omar and Brian walked toward them with their skis.

"Hey guys," Brian said. "I was studying the map. Do you want to do the runs over on this side?" he asked, pointing to a few broad pistes descending from their left.

"Sounds good to me," David said, looking at the others.

"They are strong intermediate runs, and there are some easier cut-offs here and there if Omar needs them, although he seems to be picking things up quickly," Brian noted.

Roberto murmured under his breath, "I bet he is."

They stepped onto their skis and headed off. The runs were broad and gentle, offering enough variation to challenge the experienced skiers, but not too daunting for Omar. Omar and Brian would stop periodically to rest.

"This is amazing," Omar noted, his face turned toward the sun. "It's so quiet and peaceful."

Brian looked around at the snow-laden trees, the bright blue sky, and the handsome man standing next to him. "Even one day on the slopes feels like a longer vacation. It's such a dramatic respite from the office, the city, and countless responsibilities. All one can do on the snow is focus on the next turn. When one stops for a rest, one is surrounded by beauty and tranquility."

Omar nodded. He glanced off in the distance at the ice-covered St. Lawrence River flowing at the base of the mountain. "Shall we?" he asked as he adjusted his gloves and looked ready to continue their descent.

Brian nodded and pushed off, his skis gliding quietly over the fresh packed powder snow. They met Carlos, David, and Roberto at the bottom. They agreed to do one more run. Omar felt his legs burn as he contracted his muscles with each turn. He was eager to impress his friends and pushed through the pain. At the end of the run, he sighed with relief, kicking off his skis and looking up at the mountain he had traversed. Carlos, David, and Roberto were cleaning their skis of fresh snow, loosening the buckles on their boots, and jostling with each other. Omar envied their camaraderie and wished he had friends with whom he could be himself.

He glanced at Brian, who seemed caring, attentive, and understanding. He hoped he wouldn't bore him or impede his having fun. Brian looked up as he unbuckled his boot and smiled warmly at Omar. Omar felt his heart melt.

7

Chapter Seven - The Overnight

After returning to the city from the mountain, Brian convinced Omar to join his companions for dinner. After drinks at the apartment, they bundled up and made their way down the hill to Rue Saint-Paul and to a small bistro. They went inside and the owner welcomed them, seating them in a cozy bay window facing the street.

"This is so charming, Brian. I love the beam ceilings and the fireplace and the antiques. How did you find this?" Carlos inquired.

"Someone at work recommended it. They say the food is excellent," Brian added, feeling the solidity of Omar's body pressed up against his in the tight space. He glanced at Omar and gave him a warm smile.

Roberto ordered wine for the table, and David selected several appetizers for them to share. Roberto continued to be unsettled with Omar at Brian's side, fussing nervously with the menu, and tapping his finger impatiently as the server slowly uncorked the bottle of wine.

Once everyone had a glass, Brian proposed a toast. "To a fun day on the slopes!"

They all clinked their glasses and took long sips of the dark red wine.

"So, Omar, what do you think? Did you like skiing?" Carlos inquired.

"Incredible. I thought it would be more difficult. Thanks for your patience with me."

David and Carlos nodded. Brian smiled. Roberto's face was buried in his menu. "Does anyone know what *lapin aux trois moutardes* means?" he asked impatiently, as if perturbed and disengaged from the conversation.

Omar answered, "It's rabbit with three mustards."

"Oh," Roberto said. "Hm, sounds intriguing."

"I hear it's good," Brian remarked.

The table was crowded, and Brian let his hand drop to his lap and slide toward Omar's thigh. As Omar picked at the appetizers and drank wine, he pressed closer to Brian, who, given the green light, patted Omar affectionately under the table. The touch of their bodies was electrifying, sending rushes of energy up Brian's arm and into his chest. David began a diatribe about Canadian politics, and Roberto whispered in Carlos's ear. Brian decided on an entrée and looked over at Omar. "Do you know what you want?"

Alarmed at Brian's wording, Roberto looked up, and Omar nodded. The double entendre wasn't wasted on Carlos, who chuckled nervously. He continued his earlier line of questioning. "Are you planning to ski tomorrow?" he asked Omar.

Omar looked at Brian, who answered for him. "I asked him to join us again tomorrow. He's going to play hooky from school."

"Bad boy," David said with a devilish smile.

Omar blushed. "It was a lot of fun. I can ski on my own, so I don't hold you back," he added.

"Don't be silly," David remarked. "We all have a different pace - some fast, others more cautious. It will be fine." He looked over at Brian, who picked up on the not-so-hidden message and glared at him.

Carlos then interjected, "Omar, Brian said you are studying theoretical physics. What is that?"

"It's an attempt to make sense of how things work, the primary forces of nature, things like that."

"Things like gravity, time, space – Einstein's theories?" Carlos followed with more questions.

"Yes. We're in search of unifying theories, ways of making sense of the totality of things."

"Sounds philosophical to me," Roberto noted, looking up briefly from his menu.

"There's an aspect of philosophy to it, an attempt to reconcile philosophical theories with actual observations," Omar added.

Brian looked at Omar proudly and then glanced at Roberto. Roberto was a research scientist, too, and could be cruel without restraint if he didn't like someone's scientific hypotheses. Brian gave Roberto a stern look, suggesting he restrain himself.

Roberto nodded but proceeded with a question. "I've never really understood the double-split experiment and the idea that consciousness can shape matter. It seems impossible."

"Yes. Most physicists agree – it makes little sense. But as a scientist yourself, you must know we have to follow evidence where it takes us. The evidence is there. We must adjust our theories, our understanding of how things work. We can't pretend something is what it isn't."

Roberto bristled, then continued. "But how do you reconcile that with our ability to predict material or chemical reactions – material cause and effect? That's how medicine works," Roberto noted, cocking his head back slightly.

Brian reached under the table and took Omar's hand and squeezed it. He hoped he would pick up on the message – 'don't provoke him.'

Omar looked at Brian and smiled. Then he turned toward Roberto and said confidently, "Yes, reconciling our observation of material cause and effect with some of the quantum observations that have been made is the biggest challenge in science and physics. À propos to medicine, isn't that why we test with placebos – to account for the so-called mind-body effect, the mind's ability to change conditions in the body?"

Roberto nodded approvingly. He realized Omar was a formidable scientist and not just a hot twinkie Brian had picked up. But this unnerved him more. Even though he and Brian agreed they would never be lovers, the attention he was paying to Omar disturbed him, and he was surprised by his own jealousy.

David rescued the conversation from the scientific rabbit hole to focus on more practical matters – including reservations for a dog-sled ride, tickets to visit the ice hotel, and decisions about restaurants. Roberto picked up his phone and scrolled through his dating app, hoping to find a hookup for later in the evening. If he couldn't beat Omar with science, he might remind Brian that he was missing out on a lot of local action.

The rest of the evening progressed amicably with interesting conversations, good food, abundant wine, followed by dessert and coffee. They bundled up and made their way back to the apartment. Robert announced he was heading out, presumably on a date. David and Carlos excused themselves and went back to their room. Brian invited Omar to stay for another glass of wine. They sat on the sofa in front of the fireplace, where several fresh logs were crackling in the orange flames.

"So, you liked skiing?" Brian began, wringing his hands nervously.

"Loved it," Omar replied. "I hope I wasn't too much of a drag for you and your friends?"

"Not at all. It's fun introducing someone to the sport. I think it's a great way to enjoy winter."

"I was thinking the same thing. I usually dread the cold and long winters. This is a wonderful way to enjoy the snow!"

"Precisely." Brian stared into Omar's dark, weepy eyes. He was adorable, and his child-like enthusiasm was enchanting. He leaned toward him and gave him a long, warm, moist kiss. Omar, without hesitation, kissed him back, opening his mouth wide and breathing Brian in.

Omar looked nervously around the room.

"Don't worry. Carlos and David are already asleep, and Roberto won't be back for some time."

Omar sighed, but remained anxious. Brian could feel it in Omar's hands, which he held tight. "Let's go to my room?" Brian suggested.

Omar nodded without hesitation. They walked back to Brian's room and shut the door. Brian turned on a small lamp, its soft glow filling the room.

"Are you okay?" Brian asked thoughtfully, concerned about Omar's apparent lack of much experience.

Omar nodded, reaching toward Brian and unbuttoning his shirt. He slid his hand inside the fabric and felt the soft and warm contours of Brian's chest. Brian leaned his head back and moaned.

In the subdued lighting, Omar's eyes were haunting, dark, and inviting. Brian was still fascinated with how large they were and how they narrowed toward his temples into handsome lines. He traced his fingers over Omar's brows and kissed his large, sensuous nose.

Omar removed Brian's shirt and ran his hands over his shoulders, squeezing his biceps playfully. "Surprisingly *musclé*," he whispered.

Brian smiled. "I work out."

"It shows," Omar murmured, running his hand over Brian's chest. Brian wasn't a muscle boy, but he was lean, taut, and strong. He was smooth and hairless with just enough definition that Omar began to lick the sides of his pecs with abandon.

Brian got aroused. He reached down and unzipped Omar's ski pants. "Time to get these off," he whispered. Underneath, Omar's large cock was pressing against the stretchy fabric of his long underwear. Brian reached provocatively through the fly and felt Omar's warm, soft skin. He stroked it and then pulled his hand out, slipping his fingers into the elastic waist, and pulling Omar's thermals off.

Omar didn't flinch. He reached over and unbuttoned Brian's jeans and left them hanging seductively on his hips. He reached around the back, slid his hands under Brian's undershorts and squeezed his firm, round buttocks.

Brian moaned and gave Omar a long, warm, moist kiss. He pushed Omar onto the bed. All he had on were his wool socks. Brian spread Omar's legs slightly and ran his hand up along the outside of his erection, squeezing the glans, moist now with anticipation.

Omar's torso was dark and hairy. He was lean and muscular, his pecs well-defined, and his abdomen sculpted. Brian ran his hand up Omar's stomach and playfully squeezed his pecs, hardening with desire. "Looks like someone else works out," he said, staring into Omar's deep orbs.

Brian climbed on top of Omar and ran his hand over the contours of his face. He stared at him and said, "*Quelle surprise.*"

Omar reached his legs around Brian's waist and used his feet to slide Brian's pants and underwear down. He could feel the intense heat emanating from Brian's erect and large cock pressed against his own sex.

"*Ça va?*" Brian inquired, gazing into Omar's eyes.

Omar nodded and whispered, "*Et toi?*"

"Happy," Brian said. He was startled by the word that came out of his mouth, one he never used regarding a trick. He felt something deeper than arousal, as if something was penetrating the protective shell he worked so hard to erect and maintain.

Brian sat up between Omar's legs and pressed his hard shaft against Omar's balls. Omar propped himself on his elbows and gazed at Brian hovering over him. Brian leaned down and wrapped his arms around Omar's back, pulling him up toward him. Brian wrapped his legs around Omar's waist so that their moist hot erections pressed against each other. He gave Omar a deep kiss and felt Omar's shaft quiver.

"Qu'est-ce que tu veux faire?" Brian asked, not sure what Omar's preferences might be.

"Je veux te regarder," he said sensually, surprising Brian with his sentimentality. No one had ever told him they just wanted to look at him.

Brian could feel his own hardness throb and become increasingly sensitive. He thought he might come just looking into Omar's eyes.

Omar leaned forward and kissed Brian, opening his mouth wide. They both let the intensity of their desire flow between them as their mouths moistened. Omar pulled back slightly, letting some warm saliva run down his chin. It dropped onto their erections. Brian felt the hot warmth slide down his cock, and he felt tremors of pleasure course through his body. He reached down and held his and Omar's hardness, stroking them firmly. He noticed Omar's body tighten with arousal. Suddenly, he felt pulses of heat in his hand as Omar came, shooting his load into the air. He came almost immediately afterwards, surges of pleasure and contentment coursing through his body. He collapsed onto Omar and rested his head on his shoulder.

Omar didn't move. He reached his arms around Brian's back and held him tenderly. Brian stirred, nuzzling himself into the contours of Omar's body. Omar breathed deeply. He felt a deep sense of peace, as if the clashing parts of his life had signed a truce. He felt as if his identity as a Muslim, as a scientist, and as a gay man suddenly fused together.

Brian was ordinarily quick to extract himself after sex, recompose himself, have a drink and, if the guy was hot enough, repeat. He breathed in the distinctive smell of Omar's skin and savored the feel of it against his cheek. He closed his eyes and took delight in the comforting embrace of Omar's arms. They both dozed off and woke later. After washing up, Brian took Omar's hand and led him back to the bed. They slid under the billowy duvet cover, held each other tightly, and fell back to sleep.

8

Chapter Eight – The Interloper

Roberto pressed the electronic combination on the front door of the apartment. He was drunk and had difficulty coordinating his fingers with the keypad. After a couple of attempts, the lock unlatched, and he stumbled into the living room. On the coat rack, he noticed Omar's jacket and bristled.

He threw his jacket on the back of a chair, walked into the kitchen, popped a couple of aspirin in his mouth, and drank a large glass of water. Walking down the hallway, he noticed Brian's door closed. He mumbled something under his breath and entered.

Soft orange light filtered through the slats of the shades, and Roberto could make out two bodies entwined under the covers. Brian's distinctive hair was visible over the top border of the duvet. Roberto slipped his pants and shirt off quietly and slipped in next to him. Brian stirred, but didn't wake at first. Roberto felt the heat of Brian's skin next to his and became aroused. He nuzzled his hardness into the soft space between Brian's full, round buttocks, and Brian woke.

"What the," he began, rotating now to face Roberto. "Roberto, what are you doing here?"

"Shh," Roberto said, putting his finger up to Brian's lips.

"Roberto, you're drunk and smell like smoke and other things I won't mention."

Roberto grinned. "And you smell like Morocco."

Brian pushed Roberto, who fell off the edge of the bed onto the floor. The sound woke Omar, who said, "*Qu'est-ce qui se passe?* What's going on?"

"It's okay," Brian said. "Roberto got confused and thought he was in his room."

Roberto pulled himself up and stood at the edge of the bed, his erection proudly waving in front of him. "I wasn't confused. Brian likes threesomes, and I thought I would oblige. Who's the bottom?"

"Roberto, get out of here. You're drunk, and I have no interest in a threesome."

"What's changed?"

Brian was now angry, stood up, and grabbed Roberto by the arm. He led him out into the hallway and said, "Roberto, go to your room. You're screwing this up."

"Ah, so you found a cute Arab to fuck. That's been your fantasy for a while. Sorry, I thought we could share."

Brian wanted to hit Roberto, but he figured he was drunk enough he could lead him to his room. He continued to squeeze his harm firmly, led him through the door, and pushed him onto his bed. "*Bonne nuit.*"

As Brian returned to his room, Omar was dressing. "What's up? Don't leave."

"Sorry. I need to get home."

"Don't mind Roberto. He's drunk and doesn't know what he's saying."

Omar shook his head. "That's okay. I need to get going anyway."

"What about tomorrow? I thought we were going to ski."

"Yeah. I know. There are a lot of deadlines at school. I probably should spend the day on campus."

"Please don't leave. I apologize for Roberto. He's not himself."

"He's been that way all day. I don't want to get in the way of something between you."

"You're not. There's nothing between us. Roberto and I are best friends from a long time ago. That's all."

"That's not what it seems. I had a good time. I'll text you later."

Omar tied his shoes, walked into the living room, retrieved his coat, and called for an Uber. "He's just five minutes away," he said as he glanced at his phone.

Brian went back into the bedroom, slipped on some shorts, and returned. He walked up to Omar and stared deeply into his eyes. "I had a good time. What a pleasant surprise."

Omar nodded unconvincingly. "I'll text you tomorrow. Have a good time on the slopes."

A pair of headlights pulled up in front of the house. Omar gave Brian a warm hug and kissed him on the cheeks. "À bientôt."

"Ciao," Brian replied, hanging onto Omar's hand as long as he could.

Omar left, and Brian locked the door. He went back into his room, slid under the covers, and breathed in Omar's scent. He tried to fall back asleep, but his heart was racing and his head spinning.

The next morning, Carlos and David were at the dining table sipping coffee, reading papers, and nibbling on some croissants. Brian walked in, poured himself some coffee, and sat pensively at the table.

"What was all the racket last night?"

"Sorry. The abbreviated version is that Omar stayed over, and we had a good time. Roberto came home drunk, tried to get into bed with us, and scared Omar off."

Carlos raised his eyebrow and David looked up from his iPad. David asked, "Where's Roberto?"

"Probably hung over and still in bed. That piece of shit."

"Brian, you guys are best of friends. What happened?" Carlos pressed further.

"He made Omar think I was into threesomes. I think he scared him off. I really liked him."

"You've never talked like that about your tricks," David remarked. "What's different about this one?"

Brian looked off into the distance and rubbed his chin. "I don't know. He wasn't the classic hook up. We've only spent a day together, but there's something different."

"You're scaring me," Carlos interjected. "You're my idol. You have the idyllic gay life – you're smart, good looking, have a great job, and have lots of sex. Are you thinking about settling down?"

David gave Carlos a scrutinizing look.

"No, no, no," Brian said excitedly. "*Moi*, settle down. I don't think so."

"Then why the anger at Roberto? He did you a favor."

"It felt clingy – like Roberto was clinging to me. He was acting irrational and messing up a nice affair."

David raised his brows. "Didn't you and Roberto have a thing once?"

"A long time ago. In college. It didn't work. We're great friends. *Basta*." Brian got up and went to the counter to fix a bowl of cereal.

Carlos whispered into David's ear, "Maybe Roberto wants more."

David whispered back, "Or maybe Roberto is afraid of losing Brian as a best friend."

Carlos nodded and looked inquisitively at David. "How did you get so insightful?"

A few minutes later, Roberto sauntered into the room. His hair was tousled, his eyes bloodshot, and his walk labored. Carlos stood up, poured him a big cup of coffee, handed it to him, and said, "I think you'll need this."

Roberto nodded and plopped into one of the chairs at the table.

Brian glared at him. Roberto didn't notice. His eyes were unfocused.

"So," David began, "Fun night out?"

Roberto nodded, taking a long sip of coffee. "Where's Ahmed?" he asked with a mumbled voice.

"His name is Omar, and he left," Brian said with irritation.

"So soon?" Roberto said pointedly.

"Well, you didn't exactly make him feel at home?" Brian noted.

"I was ready to embrace him with open arms, if I recall," Roberto laughed groggily.

Brian glared at him, stood up, and returned to his room. He texted Omar: "Omar. Sorry about last night. Roberto is a jerk. I had a good time. Can we talk?"

No response.

Brian undressed, turned on the shower in the bathroom and, when it was hot, stepped in and felt the soothing water caress him. He felt angry at Roberto and unsettled about Omar. Ordinarily, he would hook up with a cute guy and, if he spent the night, have breakfast, kiss, and wrap things up. There was closure. With Omar, there were a lot of loose ends.

He texted again: "Can I meet you later? I want to explain."

No response.

An hour later, Carlos and David dressed for a day on the slopes. "Are you coming?" David asked Brian.

Brian paused, looked out the window at the bright sunshine and said, "Why not? Looks like a beautiful day. Give me five minutes, and I'll be ready." He realized there wasn't much he could do about Omar, and he hoped Roberto would be too drunk to ski.

"Roberto, are you going to ski today?" David yelled down the hall.

"No," Roberto replied in a groggy voice. "I need some sleep."

"*Allons-y*," Brian suggested as he stepped into the living room with dressed in his ski pants and jacket and his boot bag in tow.

Carlos, David, and Brian drove to Mont-Sainte-Anne and made their way quickly to one of the chairlifts, making early tracks on the freshly groomed runs. Part way down the mountain, they stopped to take in the views and let the sun warm their faces. "Beautiful," Brian said, looking out over the Saint Lawrence River.

"Yes. This ski area is nicer than I imagined," Carlos noted. "I'm glad you recommended we come here. It's been great skiing and feels like a winter wonderland." He paused and then continued. "Are you okay?"

"I'm still annoyed at Roberto."

"I can imagine," David interjected.

They skied to the bottom of the run and took another chair up. On the chair, Brian asked Carlos and David, "What got into Roberto? I've never seen him like that."

David looked over at Carlos, who nodded. David began, "Have you ever considered that perhaps Roberto is in love with you?"

"That's not possible. Sure, we had a little thing in college, but it didn't work. We've been best friends. That's it. He does his thing. I do mine. If he was in love, why would he share all the details about his tricks?"

David looked off into the distance. He turned toward Brian and said, "This is just a thought. Maybe Roberto needs you."

"Needs me?"

"Yes. Maybe you're not lovers, but as long as you are just tricking guys, he knows he is your best friend, that you need him, and that he can confide in you."

"I don't get it," Brian said.

"Think about it. As long as you're not serious about anyone, the two of you are close. If you get close to someone else, he thinks he will lose you as his best friend."

"But if I'm with someone else, it won't change the fact that we are best friends."

"He doesn't know that. It will inevitably change your friendship, and that's scary for him."

Brian nodded. "Hm. Maybe you're right. But that doesn't change how angry I am."

"Why are you so angry?"

"He messed things up with Omar."

"What things?" David pressed further.

Brian couldn't answer. He was in unfamiliar territory, and he was unable to articulate how he felt. He was grateful the chair lift arrived at the terminus, and they unloaded. They began skiing down the mountain, taking some of the easier intermediate slopes to warm up. Brian was lost in thought, and occasionally had to remind himself to focus on the terrain. They arrived at the gondola station at the bottom of the mountain and took another ride up. Carlos and David got distracted by a text from friends in Atlanta, and Brian used the occasion to check to see if Omar had replied to his earlier texts. He hadn't.

They continued to ski and later, in the afternoon, returned to the apartment, where they found Roberto sleeping on the sofa in front of the fireplace. Carlos and David took a nap, and Brian texted Omar once more. "Omar. Can we talk?"

No response.

Later, they went out to eat. Brian was annoyed with Roberto, but the conversation amongst the four of them was cordial. Roberto had recovered from his hangover and was his customary gregarious self. Brian was quiet and kept eyeing a cute French man at the bar. As they finished dinner and bundled up for the walk home, Brian stopped at the bar and said, "I like your sweater. Did you get it here locally? I'm looking for a nice store."

The man smiled and said, "*Je m'appelle Etienne.*"

"*Brian. Enchanté.*"

"The store is nearby. Shall I show you?"

"Show me anything you want," Brian said provocatively.

Brian waved to his friends, who winked at him. Etienne paid his tab, put on his coat, and grabbed Brian's arm, saying, "This way."

A few hours later, Brian returned to find Carlos and David in bed, as expected, and Roberto sitting by the fireplace, nursing a glass of wine.

"Nice night out?" Roberto inquired.

"Eh, it was okay. And you?"

"Quiet. I needed a break. You want to join me?"

Brian nodded. He took off his coat, went to the bathroom, poured a glass of wine in the kitchen, and sat in a large comfortable chair near the fireplace.

"Are we okay?" Roberto began.

"Not sure. I was very annoyed with what you did to Omar."

"I know. I was a dick."

Brian nodded.

"I've been thinking," Roberto continued. "Maybe we should give it another go."

Brian looked at Roberto. "Are you kidding?"

"No. I've given it some thought. I think I was jealous of you and Omar and realized perhaps we have more here than we think."

"You know what happened before. We haven't changed. We'd run into the same issues."

"Maybe not. Maybe we can make it work."

"I don't think so," Brian said emphatically. "I treasure our friendship, and I want to assure you that whatever happens, you and I will be best friends."

Robert's eyes watered. "That means a lot. I think I was afraid I would lose you. I've never seen you the way you were with Omar."

Brian looked off into the distance. "It does seem different, doesn't it?"

Roberto nodded. "What is it?"

"I don't know. It creeped up and took hold of me. I wasn't expecting it."

"What do you like about him?"

"I don't know. We just met. I get a feeling – a sense of compatibility. We're both scientists, growing up in conservative religious families. We come from different ethnic and linguistic worlds, yet there's a connection, a bridge that traverses the expanse."

Roberto was still sad, but he got up and walked toward Brian's chair. He sat on the arm and wrapped his arm around Brian's neck. "I love you. I don't want to lose you as a friend. If you can assure me of that, I'll support whomever you settle down with."

"Who says I'm settling down?"

"You just did – not in those exact words – but it's there. He's the one."

Brian wiped the tears from his own eyes. He had wanted love and acceptance so much. He realized Roberto loved him unconditionally, and now he wondered if Roberto was right, that Omar was more than a cute short-term hook up.

They sat in front of the fire, gazing at the burning embers and sitting with their thoughts. They didn't need to say anything more. It was there – a sense of security, peace, and affection, one that wouldn't wane with time.

9

Chapter Nine - Boston

Two weeks later, Brian's phone pinged with a text from Omar: "Brian. I hope you are well. Sorry I have been out of touch. I have an appointment in Cambridge next week. Would you like to meet?"

Brian, shocked, re-read the text a couple of times and then replied: "Good to hear from you. Yes, I would like to see you. Let me know when a good time might be – perhaps for a drink or dinner."

Omar responded: "What about next Thursday? Dinner? Let me know when and where."

Brian thought a second and then replied: "Il Vinoteca – in the North End. Seven o'clock?"

"Perfect. I'll find it." Omar replied. "*À bientôt.*"

The following Thursday, Brian was a nervous wreck. He had difficulty concentrating on work, had butterflies in his stomach, and kept revising in his head what he wanted to say and what he hoped might unfold. He arrived early at the restaurant. The owners and servers knew him and gave him an excellent table near a cozy window looking out onto the busy street in Boston's iconic Italian neighborhood. He ordered a glass of wine and checked emails while he waited for Omar.

Brian glanced out the window and saw Omar walking toward the restaurant. He was bundled up for the unusually cold evening. Light snow was falling. Omar walked past the window, waved at Brian, and entered the front door. A server took his coat and glanced toward Brian. Omar weaved his way through the crowded dining area. Brian stood, reached toward him, and gave him a warm embrace. They both exchanged kisses on the cheek and sat down.

"I'm so glad you reached out. It's great to see you again," Brian began, beaming with excitement.

"*Pareillement*," Omar agreed in French, nervously avoiding eye contact.

There was a protracted silence as they each searched for an appropriate beginning. Brian gazed into Omar's large, beautiful brown eyes. His thick, dark lashes were slightly moist as he adjusted to the warmth inside the restaurant. His dark hair glowed in the dimmed overhead lights, and his lips were full and deep red. He looked even more delicious than Brian recalled.

Omar shifted nervously as Brian continued to gaze into his eyes. He felt bad that he hadn't responded to Brian's emails in Quebec. He glanced evasively across the room and then said, "Nice place. Do you come here often?"

"Yes. I'm a regular. I live nearby. I like the North End. It has an old-world charm to it, and the Italian restaurants are great. This is my favorite."

Omar slowly began to relax. Brian had a calming countenance to him, and as they settled into a conversation, Omar's pulse returned to normal. He wasn't sure what he hoped to accomplish meeting Brian. On the one hand, he remained curious. What would it be like to embark on a longer-term relationship, something more than a hook-up or a sordid obsession with someone unattainable? The connection he felt with Brian intrigued him, and he wanted to test it out. On the other hand, he feared the implications of a substantial relationship, one that might force him to come out. He wasn't sure he was ready. Omar looked directly at Brian and realized he needed to apologize. He said, "I'm sorry for the lack of my response. I was uncomfortable and not sure how to proceed. In fact, I'm still uncertain."

Brian interpreted Omar's reticence as something connected with Robert's intrusion and replied, "I'm sorry for Roberto's behavior. It was inappropriate."

Omar looked evasively down at the table and nervously rotated his fork. "It wasn't just Roberto."

Defensively, Brian added, "For what it's worth, I don't do threesomes."

Omar grinned. "I hoped that was the case. I am not comfortable coming out, particularly with my conservative religious family, and the last thing I need is to get involved in something like that." Omar took a deep breath, hesitant to utter what was to follow. In his head he said to himself, 'Oh what the fuck, let it out.' "I think I panicked because I liked you. I found you interesting, charming, affable. It was scary."

Brian's eyes widened at Omar's declaration. Omar had voiced his own apprehension. He was scared, too. He was entering unchartered territory, a place he vowed he wouldn't enter after Eric left him.

"I can appreciate and understand that. I had a nice time with you – however brief – and I would like to get to know you more," Brian said, amazed at the words coming out of his mouth. He had male friends who he saw regularly, but since Eric, he had never pursued a long-term romantic relationship. It was just too fraught with peril and uncertainty.

They both stared at each other awkwardly, uncomfortably.

"And Roberto? How is he?" Omar asked, finding it easier to focus on a third party.

"Funny you should ask. We had a long conversation after that evening. I think he feared he was losing me as a friend when he saw how well you and I were getting along."

Omar shuffled nervously in his chair.

Brian stared at him, trying to get a read. He realized they had spent less than two days together. How was it possible that Roberto or anyone could have thought they were hitting it off, getting along, progressing toward something more serious? Had he overstated things?

"Sorry. I didn't mean to be presumptuous," Brian apologized.

"You weren't," Omar said emphatically, without elaboration. Then he added, "Things were going nicely. I was just frightened."

"I get it. I would have been, too."

"Again, it wasn't just Roberto. I am not sure I'm ready."

"There's no hurry," Brian interjected, realizing Omar was fighting a battle within himself.

Brian took a sip of wine. He wasn't sure how to proceed. Thankfully, Omar asked, "So, how's your work?"

"Good. Busy."

"Any interesting projects?"

"Always," Brian said without elaboration. Most of their research was confidential, so he couldn't disclose much. "And your studies?"

Omar picked up the not-so-subtle message that work was confidential and answered Brian's question. "Good. I defended the thesis. So officially, I'm a doctor."

"Well, then we have to celebrate!" Brian waved to the server and looked at Omar. "Prosecco?"

Omar nodded.

Brian continued, "I didn't realize you were so close to finishing when we met."

"It was more of a formality at that point. I had completed the thesis work, had defended it, and was waiting for the approval from the department."

"Well, that's amazing! You seemed so calm. I would have been on pins and needles waiting for the verdict."

The waiter came, poured Prosecco into fluted glasses, and they raised them. Brian said, "*Félicitations!*"

"*Merci*," Omar replied. They both took sips of the bubbly liquid.

"Doctor Aziz! That has a nice ring to it," Brian said. "So, what's next?"

"I have to find work. Although my field is theoretical physics, there's a lot I can do on the practical side, combining teaching with new technology."

"Any ideas?"

Omar shook his head evasively. He was in Boston for a job interview, but it was confidential. He imagined Brian could have guessed he might be in town for work, but he decided not to say anything. There was a new project at MIT in quantum technology, and he had been aggressively recruited. The idea of moving to the States was appealing, but Boston was not far enough from Sherbrooke if he were to get involved with someone.

"Maybe I can ask around at work and see if my colleagues know of any positions in your field," Brian offered.

"That would be nice," Omar said. Brian detected Omar's hesitation.

"Well, should we order dinner? I assume you like Italian since you seduced me over a pizza in Quebec."

Omar blushed, still not comfortable with such direct and unfiltered reference to their *petit rancard*.

"The pasta is homemade and delicious. Their meat dishes are incredible as well, particularly the *osso buco* and the *filetto di manzo*."

"Are they *halal?*" Omar asked, grinning. He was ordinarily stoic and cerebral. Brian inspired him to dig deep for his playful side.

"Am I?" Brian asked, playing along with Omar's attempt at levity.

Omar frowned, and Brian realized his statement only reminded Omar of how far he was sliding away from his faith, his family, and their traditions.

"Sorry," Brian said. "I should be more respectful."

"It's my fault. I'm overly sensitive."

Brian thought to himself that Omar was facing a major cross-roads in his life. He had finished his studies and was expected to find a job, settle down, and start a family. For most graduate students, the choices were straightforward. For Omar, coming to terms with his sexuality complicated things immensely.

Brian gazed into Omar's eyes with a look of tenderness and compassion. Omar could sense Brian's understanding. It was reassuring.

"So, what should we order?" Brian asked, looking over at the menu lying on the side of the table.

"I think I'll have the bolognese. And you?"

"I'm craving the filet. Would you have some if I order it?"

Omar nodded. The idea of their sharing meals felt peculiarly erotic, as if it embodied something much more, the dropping of barriers and the embrace of intimacy with a man.

They continued to visit. Both found it easy to talk with one another, discovering they had more in common than their academic backgrounds. Both loved books, movies, and theater. Omar loved going with his parents and Hakim to New York to see Broadway plays. Brian thought it odd given their religious proclivities and the irreverent themes of many shows.

They shifted back and forth between languages. Brian loved the way Omar's mouth pursed as he spoke French. His face would become more playful and sexier, and his hands more animated as well.

They both recounted amusing stories about dates with women gone bad, and they lamented the absence of dating opportunities amongst the nerdy male graduate students who seemed out-of-touch with their sexuality.

Their entrees came, and they devoured them with abandon, both hungry from a long day of work and Omar's stressful interview, which he continued to keep under wraps. They passed their plates back and forth, and reached their forks across the table, taking morsels of food off each other's plates. Omar felt himself vacillate between a sense of calm and familiarity with Brian, as if they were old friends, and an intensifying buzz as passion-induced adrenaline raced through his system. Periodically, his body would tremble as he felt Brian's allure.

The restaurant emptied, many patrons rushing off to a Bruins-Canadiens hockey game in the nearby Boston Garden.

"Dessert?" Brian asked as they settled into a second bottle of wine.

Omar nodded, relieved at the prospect of more time with Brian. They ordered a chocolate torte and two espressos. As they were waiting, Brian placed his hand next to Omar's. Omar could feel the heat emanating from it and placed his hand on top of Brian's. He gazed into Brian's eyes and felt so at home and comfortable expressing affection.

Brian looked down at their entwined hands. It was an endearing gesture; one long-term lovers would share. Brian felt his pulse race and his heart pound nervously. He had crossed a line. There was no turning back. He had allowed his heart to beat eagerly for someone. Against all his self-imposed controls, he began to utter softly and tenderly, "*Je t'aime.*"

Omar raised his brows. It was an astonishing declaration so early in their interaction, but it didn't entirely surprise him. He felt it too. Encouraged, he said, "*Moi aussi.*"

Brian stroked the top of Omar's hand with one of his fingers and looked out the window at the snowfall. Standing just outside and staring at them were two men. They looked Arab, and they had Canadiens hockey jerseys on. Omar followed Brian's gaze. He let out a gasp and quickly withdrew his hand. "*Merde*," he murmured.

The two men entered, and Brian grew alarmed. Omar stood and embraced them, saying, "*Quelle surprise!*" They nodded. He turned to Brian and said, "Brian, these are my cousins, Tariq and Hassan. Tariq and Hassan, this is Brian. He is a research scientist here in Boston who I am consulting for my doctoral work."

"*Enchanté*," Tariq said, scrutinizing Brian carefully.

Brian said in return, "*Enchanté.*" He looked at Omar inquisitively. He then continued, "Looks like you are here for the game with the Bruins."

"Yes. As you know, there's a good rivalry between the Habs and the Boston Bruins," Hassan noted, carefully looking at Omar. "We had some business in town and decided to go to the game," he added.

Omar then said, "Don't let us delay you. We are just finishing dinner."

"Yes. We saw. Looks like you're having dessert," Tariq said with irony, raising his eyebrow. He didn't smile, and his consternation wasn't missed by Omar, who just nodded.

"When are you heading back to Sherbrooke? Do you need a ride?"

"I still have some meetings here in Boston," Omar lied. "And, I have my own car," Omar noted nervously. Tariq and Hassan continued to look at him and at Brian intensely, trying to determine the real agenda.

"Well, safe travels," Tariq said.

"You, too," Brian replied. They hugged, and Tariq and Hassan left and continued toward the game.

"Shit, shit, shit," Omar said, his face flush and his hand trembling.

"What's wrong?" Brian said. "Why don't we sit?"

"Do you think they saw us – just a few moments ago – you know, with my hand on yours?"

"I don't know. It's possible."

"Tariq and Hassan are cut from the same cloth as Hakim. They are conservative and homophobic. If they suspect anything about us, they will go directly to their father, who will go to mine. What a disaster."

Omar looked like he was on the verge of crying. He rubbed his hands nervously through his hair and massaged his forehead.

"Don't jump the gun yet. It's possible they didn't see anything or, if they did, you can spin the story in such a way that it confirms what you told them earlier, that you were consulting a famous scientist in Boston."

"I didn't say famous," he said, not amused.

"Just tell them that I had lost a family member tragically, and that you were trying to console me."

"But if they tell their father and somehow Hakim finds out and finds out it's you, it will be difficult to dissuade them that I'm not gay. There's too much circumstantial evidence."

"Well, maybe it's time to come out." As Brian finished his statement, he wished he could have taken it back. It wasn't what Omar needed to hear.

Omar turned ashen. He felt his legs grow week and the room begin to spin. Shaking, he said, "I can't. It would be a disaster. I'll either get beat up or cut off from the family or both."

"You've mentioned that once before. Do you really fear they would be physically abusive?"

Omar nodded nervously. He wrung his hands. He slumped in his seat. Brian could see the defeat in his eyes.

"Do you want to come to my place? We can talk."

"No. I've got to go. I think I'll head back to Sherbrooke tonight."

"I thought you said you have some meetings tomorrow."

"I just said that to get my cousins off my back," Omar said, continuing to look nervously around the room.

"You can't go back tonight. It's dangerous. There's snow, it's late, and you've had a lot of wine."

"I have so much adrenaline running through my system that I'll be up all night. I'll be okay. If I get back tonight, there will be less suspicion."

Omar had planned to return to Sherbrooke the next day to stay with his parents, and it was unlikely he would actually go there tonight. But he just couldn't go to Brian's apartment. That would be giving into Tariq and Hassan's suspicions. Even if they were true, Omar continued to play games in his own mind as if his not going to Brian's proved he wasn't gay.

"I'm worried about you," Brian said.

"Don't be. I'll be okay."

Brian asked for and paid the check. They bundled up and walked outside. Omar's car was parked in a nearby garage. They walked quietly. Brian didn't know what to say to console Omar, who seemed lost in another world, undoubtedly rehearsing in his mind all sorts of scenarios of his return home and eventual reckoning with his family.

When they got to his car, Brian took Omar's arms and held them firmly. "It will be okay. You'll see."

Omar shook his head.

"Text me when you get home," Brian added emphatically.

Omar nodded. They embraced. Omar got into his car and drove off.

10

Chapter Ten - Missing

Brian stirred, realizing he hadn't heard from Omar. He glanced at his phone and noticed it was two in the morning. There were no texts. He was now officially worried. He sent a text to Omar: "Did you make it home okay?"

There was no response. He dozed off and woke again at four. The text he had sent earlier had been delivered, but Omar hadn't responded. He fell back to sleep. At seven, he rose and got ready for work. At work, he called Omar. The call went immediately into voicemail. He left a message for him to call back.

Later that afternoon, he still hadn't heard from Omar. He had a bad feeling in the pit of his stomach. Something was wrong. Either he had an accident, or he was having trouble with his family, or perhaps both. He left work early, went home, and sat quietly.

Around eight, his phone rang. The origin of the call was the Province of Quebec, and he picked it up right away and said, "Omar?"

"No, this is Hakim. Is this Brian?"

"Hm. Yes, this is Brian. Hakim, how did you get my number? What's wrong?"

"Your number was on the invoice from the repair work. Omar hasn't returned from Boston. Two of his cousins mentioned they saw the two of you. Everyone is worried and upset. He doesn't respond to texts or calls. We wondered if you have been in touch with him."

"Oh my God," Brian murmured to himself. "Hakim, the last I heard from him was when he left last night for Sherbrooke. I tried to dissuade him, but he insisted on returning. I have tried texting and calling with no response, either. Do you think he had an accident?"

"I think if he had an accident, we would have been notified by the police, who would have checked his identity."

"Yes, you're probably right. So, what do you think is up?"

"If it were my guess, he's afraid to face his family. Tariq and Hassan have been making a lot of trouble about him, saying you two were having a romantic dinner, that Omar is gay, that he's an embarrassment for the family."

Brian didn't know how to respond. He remained quiet.

"Brian, are you still there?"

"Yes, Hakim. I'm here. I don't know what to say."

"We need to find him before he does something tragic."

"Has someone checked his apartment at Laval?"

"Yes, my daughter did. No one is there. The neighbors haven't seen him, either."

"Hm. So what do you think?"

"We were hoping you might have some ideas."

"Sorry. I'm as perplexed as you."

"If you hear anything, will you let us know?"

"Of course," he said.

Just as he and Hakim were about to hang up, Brian interjected. "Hakim, hold on. Are Omar's credit cards or debit cards linked to anyone's account – like his father's? If so, you could check to see if there have been any charges? We could find out where he is."

"That's a great idea. I'll call his father and see. In the meantime, let us know if you hear from him."

Hakim and Brian hung up. Brian started pacing his apartment and murmured, "Omar, Omar, Omar – call. Get in touch with someone."

Brian felt horrible. He feared he had pressed Omar too much and had inadvertently gotten him into trouble with his family. The reality of what was happening triggered his own traumatic memories, and he began to shake. He felt flush and sweaty. Even though he had overcome the estrangement from his family, he realized it would be formidable for Omar, perhaps worse given the tight-knit clan he was part of.

The next afternoon, Hakim called. "Brian. Omar's father went to the bank. His account is independent and private, but the banker, who is a close family friend, was willing to log into his account and see if there had been any activity. Sure enough, they discovered he had purchased a plane ticket to Morocco."

"Morocco?" Brian exclaimed. "Why Morocco?"

"We have no idea. We don't have any relatives we are in touch with, and he has only been there once as a child."

Omar's travel to Morocco stumped Brian. Omar was neither religious nor sentimental about his origins. Why would he go to Morocco and why so secretively?

"Any other charges?"

"A hotel in Montreal. He must have gone there instead of to his parents' the other day."

"Does anyone have a key to his apartment? Perhaps they can see if there are any clues about why he would travel to Morocco."

"I'll have my daughter check right away. She knows where a key is hidden."

Three hours later, Hakim called. "Brian. My daughter found some envelopes with a return address in Rabat. The name was a certain Aman Hadi. We looked him up. He's a Sufi Shaykh and a professor."

"Maybe Omar has been corresponding with him about his doctoral work. Maybe he decided to pay him a visit, put a little distance between him and his family."

Hakim didn't respond immediately, but then said, "That makes some sense."

"Hakim, did the banker notice any hotel charges in Morocco?"

"No. At least not yet. There was another charge in Morocco, but it was an unremarkable name, an unrecognizable account. It was for a small amount of money, three hundred dollars."

"Maybe it was for an apartment rental for a couple of nights. Does the charge on the account show the date of the flight?"

"Yes. It is for tomorrow. He will be in Morocco the following day."

"Hakim, can I make a proposal?"

"Yeah, sure."

"What would you think if I went to Morocco to find him?"

Hakim didn't respond at first. He cleared his throat and said, "You would do that?"

"Yes. I'm very worried about him. It's the least I could do."

"His father is making plans to fly there now."

"Maybe he should hold off. The last person Omar wants to see is his father. That's why he left without letting anyone know where he was."

"Maybe I can convince his father to hold off. But do you think he wants to see you? He hasn't been in touch."

"Probably not, but I'm less threatening than his father."

"You're right. But how are you going to find him?"

"We have one clue – the Shaykh. Did the envelope have any more information?"

"Apparently, he's at the Mohammed V university. He's a scientist."

"Bingo!" Brian replied enthusiastically.

"What?"

"Oh, it's an expression we use in English to mean we scored. We have hit our target. If we have the name of this professor and how to locate him, we'll locate Omar."

"I hope you're right. When could you go?"

"I can leave tomorrow. I can get a connecting flight through London."

"God bless you."

"I'll keep in close contact with you."

11

Chapter Eleven - Rabat

Brian glanced out of the plane window. The coast of France was visible to his left and eventually gave way to the snowy peaks of the Pyrenees. He wanted to watch the landscape passing below but kept fighting the heaviness of his eyes. Four shots of espresso at Heathrow weren't sufficient to overcome a busy twenty-four hours – tying up loose ends at work, packing, and boarding a late-night flight to London.

The plane continued its progress toward Morocco, passing over dry expanses of western Spain and eventually banking over the Atlantic toward Rabat. As the plane descended, Brian became more anxious. He wondered if his decision to search for Omar had been an impulsive mistake. It seemed reasonable and urgent yesterday, but now felt meddling and sophomoric. What did he hope to accomplish? How would Omar react when they met? Was he setting himself up for more disappointment?

After landing and disembarking, Brian cleared passport control, retrieved his luggage, and headed out of the small airport terminal to the line of taxis. The dry heat was a dramatic contrast to the icy cold he left in Boston. He stuffed his coat into his suitcase and let the warm sunshine caress his face. It had been a long journey – from Boston to London and then a connecting flight to Rabat. A weathered old man wearing a dingy suit approached him and offered a taxi ride. He smiled. Many of his teeth were missing.

"I need to go to the Sofitel," Brian said.

"*Tout de suite*," the old man said, taking Brian's bag and dropping it into the trunk.

They sped off and cruised a highway skirting the old part of Rabat and headed toward the government and educational zone of the city. The town was more modern than Brian had expected, but it seemed tired, as if it had enjoyed a rebirth at some point but lost steam.

Brian had always dreamed of visiting Morocco. It had an exotic appeal, a land shrouded in the mystery of ancient Berber tribes, conquering Arab empires, and the blending of Muslim and Jewish communities that settled on the African side of the Mediterranean after the Catholic monarchs expelled them from the Iberian Peninsula. He envisaged white-washed stone medinas, palm trees, deserts, mountain ranges, and soft breezes blowing off the ocean. As he sat in the back of the taxi observing the passing landscape, he felt an unsettled knot in the pit of his stomach, the growing apprehension of something foreboding, of secrets about Omar he wasn't sure he wanted to uncover.

They exited the highway and pulled into a nicely landscaped complex with palm trees and a luxurious hotel set at the end of a verdant promenade. Brian was met by an attentive staff who took his bags and escorted him to the front desk. As he walked inside the hotel, he smiled broadly at the elegant space with marble floors, decorative tile, luscious tropical plants set in colossal pots, fountains, and plush lounge areas. He felt like he had stepped onto a movie set with Bogart and Bergman and fully expected to rub elbows with spies at the bar. The fact that he was tracking down a missing scientist from Quebec only heightened the intrigue. He checked in, unpacked, showered, and went downstairs to have something to eat.

He had never been to Morocco and, as far as he was aware, Omar and Hakim were the only Moroccans he knew. He was puzzled by the mix of facial features and wasn't entirely sure how to categorize them. He had looked up the history of the country and realized there were strong Berber and Arab roots mixed with European influences. Omar and his family had Iberian features, undoubtedly with ancestral roots in Moorish Andalusia. Omar's caramel skin, wavy hair, and broad forehead and high cheek bones were evidence of that. The hotel staff was dominated by Berber influences, with darker skin, shorter dark hair, and rounder faces. They were handsome, but Brian kept searching for Omar's eyes.

He texted him again: "Omar. Please respond. I'm in Rabat."

The text didn't look like it was delivered. He presumed Omar's phone was turned off.

The dining room was filled with a mix of couples on vacation and businessmen meeting to discuss deals. Everyone dressed formally, and Brian felt out-of-place in his jeans and casual sweater. He was grateful for the ubiquity of French being used throughout the dining area, and ordered fresh seafood, salad, and crisp white wine. After lunch, he returned to his room, fired up his laptop, and looked up Professor Hadi. He found his number on the university directory and dialed it.

"*Allô*," a man responded on the other end.

"*Bonjour. Je suis Brian. Brian LeBlanc.*"

"*Qui?*"

"*Brian LeBlanc. Je suis un ami de Omar, Omar Aziz.*"

There was silence on the other end of the line. Finally, the man said in English, "I don't know who you are talking about."

"My friend in Quebec City, Omar Aziz, has been corresponding with you. He is missing, and we are hoping to find him. You are our only connection."

"I do recall an Omar Aziz. Yes. I received a few letters from him."

"Did he come to visit you?"

Brian detected a slight hesitation before the professor said emphatically, "No. I haven't had any visitors recently, certainly not from Quebec."

"Can I leave my number in case he contacts you?"

"Certainly," the professor replied.

Brian gave him his number and hung up. Brian's gut told him the professor wasn't being entirely truthful and decided to go to the university himself. He walked downstairs to the concierge, got directions, and headed off in a taxi. The route passed through a contemporary part of the city with modest size apartments and commercial buildings interspersed with government agencies, schools, and embassies.

The driver left him off at the main part of the campus. He consulted the directory and located Professor Hadi's building. He wandered down a hallway, found his room, and pressed his ear against the door. There was no sound inside. He knocked, but no one responded.

"Now what do I do?" Brian asked himself out loud. He sat in the garden outside the building to see if he might spot Omar making a visit. He passed some time observing local students who, for the most part, looked like their counterparts at other universities in Quebec City, Boston, or London. Coeds chatted, carried backpacks filled with books, and took time to enjoy the fresh air and sunshine between classes.

Brian remained unnerved by Omar's lack of response, glancing frequently at his phone. He felt a heaviness in his stomach and wasn't sure if it was concern about Omar's safety or a physical reaction to his own conflicting emotions. Why was he sitting in a desert in North Africa like a teenager, hoping to spot a lover? He found it difficult to make sense of the fact that he had spent years avoiding the sentiment of love but had so effortlessly told Omar, 'I love you.' Where was this heading? What did he want to happen?

He remained outside until classes ended and the campus emptied. He returned to the hotel.

Hakim texted: "Have you found Omar yet?"

Brian: "*Pas encore.* I located the professor's office. I'm sure we'll spot him sooner than later."

Hakim: "Keep me posted."

Brian: "*D'accord.*"

Shaykh Hadi was alarmed when Brian had called earlier. He returned to his home. He dialed the minister of science, Murad.

"*Alló,*" Murad responded.

"Murad, this is Hadi. We have a problem. I think MIT sent someone here to follow Omar, to stop him."

"How would they know he is here?"

"I asked myself the same question."

"What do we do?" Murad asked, his labored breath audible on the line.

"Do you have someone that can trail the guy from Boston? See what he's up to? Omar was instructed not to turn on his phone, and he's staying in a discreet residence. I am hoping the people from MIT will not be able to locate him."

"Let's hope so. I will put a team on him now. Where's he staying? What's his name?"

"Brian LeBlanc. At the Sofitel."

"*Francophone?*"

"*Oui.*"

An hour later, Murad's agents dialed Brian's number at the Sofitel. He responded. "*Allô.*"

"Brian? Brian LeBlanc?"

"*Oui. Qui parle?*"

"*Un ami d'Omar. Est-ce que vous voudriez me rejoindre dans le bar de l'hotel?*"

Brian paused. It was odd that someone would introduce themselves as Omar's friend and offer to meet him at the bar, but it was the only link or clue he had so far other than the professor.

"Yes. I'll meet you downstairs in an hour."

Murad's agents had no intention of meeting Brian. They wanted to get a physical impression of him so they could trail him. Brian went to the bar, looked around for a single male, and saw no one. The agent and his partner sat in lounge chairs nearby, pretending to be deep in conversation. They got several photos of Brian, stood, shook hands as if concluding a deal, and walked out of the front of the building.

Brian had a drink at the bar but, after an hour, concluded something had gone amiss. He paid his tab and asked the concierge where some good restaurants might be. The concierge directed him to the Rabat Medina. He took a cab and was let off near the Kasbah de Udayas, an ancient citadel on the mouth of the river near the Atlantic. The late evening light reflecting off the ocean gave the stone walls a beautiful vermillion color.

There were crowds of people taking strolls and gazing out at the breathtaking sunset. Brian scrutinized the crowd, hoping he might spot Omar by some remote stroke of luck. He crossed a busy street and headed into the Medina. It was typical of north African settlements with a maze of narrow pathways separating low-rise houses surrounding shaded courtyards and fountains.

Murad's agents trailed him. Brian got nervous as the sun set and the district became dark. The maze of passageways was disorienting, and he could feel his heart accelerate as he realized how easy it would be to get lost. He heard footsteps behind him and glanced over his shoulder. Murad's agents slipped into a small alleyway to avoid detection.

Brian made a few turns and ended on the periphery of the Medina, sighing in relief that he had exited the maze. He spotted a charming restaurant with outdoor seating and took a table with a view of the passing crowd. The warm but dry air was soothing, and Brian could feel the tension in his shoulders loosen.

The setting was part of his Moroccan fantasy - an open-aired courtyard with decorative tile pavement, Moorish architectural elements, and tropical plants. The wait staff were attentive and courteous. Most of the people were straight couples, undoubtedly having a romantic dinner together. But two men who had been seated just after him caught his attention. They seemed an odd pairing for the restaurant – overly dressed and conversing awkwardly, as if they had little to say to each other, just putting in time.

In any other situation, he would have been intrigued and seen them as potential hookups. But in Morocco, he was on guard, not wanting to get in trouble in a decidedly homophobic country. He decided to look busy, took the iPad out of his shoulder bag, and began to read.

The food was delicious - Mediterranean vegetables, grains, and fresh seafood. No alcohol was served, so he sipped tea as he dipped flatbread in an assortment of soft hummus. He finished dinner, paid his tab, and called for a taxi to bring him back to the hotel.

Once inside the hotel, he made his way to the bar for a glass of wine. He glanced at his phone. No response from Omar. A couple of businessmen were consuming generous glasses of brandy and looked toward him as he took a set at the marble counter. The barman glanced up, and Brian ordered a glass of red wine. A couple entered the bar area and took seats near him. They nodded to Brian. They were casually dressed. The man wore light slacks and a dark blue cotton pullover. He had dark wavy hair, a large nose, deep set dark eyes, and a light growth of a beard. His female companion wore dark jeans and a colorful print blouse with a decorative gem necklace and large ear pendants. She had dark hair, luminous skin, and deep red lipstick.

They both ordered drinks and were speaking to each other in French. Brian assumed they were from France, perhaps on vacation or business. Brain listened in. They spoke of their children, work, and plans for excursions to Casablanca and Marrakesh. He thought he picked up that they were from Lyon. In fact, they were from the States, working for US intelligence, and pretending to be French tourists.

The man excused himself to go to the bathroom. The woman glanced over at Brian and nodded.

He nodded back and extended his hands. *"Je m'appelle Brian."*

"Deborah," she said in response. *"Enchantée."*

"Enchanté," Brian replied in return. *"Vous êtes en vacances?"*

"Oui, on aime le Maroc. Et vous?

"Moi aussi," Brian replied, noting he was also on vacation. It was easier to explain than the fact that he was searching for a missing scholar.

"Vous venez d'où?"

"Boston," Brian replied to her question of his origins.

"Qu'est-ce que vous faites à Boston?" Deborah asked Brian, a more direct question about his work, but one she assumed he would answer without hesitation since she had painted such a casual picture of her reasons for being in Morocco.

"Je suis un chercheur medical," Brian shared.

"Impressive," Deborah replied in perfect English. "Do you work with one of the biopharmaceutical companies there?"

Her familiarity with Boston's rising prominence in the biomedical sciences and her flawless English surprised Brian. He nodded but didn't elaborate.

Deborah raised her eyebrow, realizing he must be well-positioned if he was being discreet.

"And you?"

"A teacher."

"And your husband?"

"He's not my husband. He's my brother. We are here on a research project for a book he's writing on North Africa."

"Ah," Brian said. "Is he a professor?"

"Yes. Although he's on sabbatical, in between positions."

"Do you have any suggestions for things to see while here?" Brian asked.

"Well, it depends on what you want to see and what you are looking for," she said with a bit of irony, lost on Brian.

"I'm on a quick trip. Just a brief respite from the cold of Boston. I'm really without an agenda."

Deborah's eyes widened. "If you are a medical researcher, have you made plans to visit some of the universities here? The government has been investing heavily in that area. My brother has some contacts. We could introduce you. What's your area of expertise?"

Brian realized Deborah and her brother might be an unexpected conduit to Professor Hadi, if they knew him. "Well, most of my work is in new vaccines, but I am interested in some of the crossover applications of quantum physics and biochemistry. Do you know anyone in the physics arena?"

"I'll have to ask my brother. He knows many people. I'm just tagging along."

Deborah took a long sip of her drink and glanced over the rim of her glass. Her brother, who was really another agent, was standing behind a lattice wall waiting for a signal. She raised a finger, and he retreated. It would have been difficult to show up at a bar and start chatting with Brian without being suspected of prostitution or other nefarious things. Her so-called brother offered her cover. He could leave, and she could offer excuses for him. What was important was that her target suspect nothing.

Deborah proceeded with her line of inquiry. "So, what's quantum physics?"

In the simplest layperson terms, Brian described some theories behind quantum physics. Deborah pretended to be interested and knew this was the kind of information both the Moroccan and American governments wanted to know. She worked for the Americans but, occasionally, she would freelance for the Moroccans. The US didn't want vital scientific information to be siphoned off to the Saudis, and the Moroccans didn't want MIT to steal their prize recruit, Omar.

When Brian paused and took a sip of his wine, Deborah glanced down at her phone and said, "Ah, Pierre had to take a call in the room. I'm sorry to have bothered you." She looked as if she were about to ask for the check and take her leave.

"It's no bother," Brian replied. "It's nice to have someone to talk with. But I don't want to keep you from whatever you and Pierre had planned."

"We were just killing time."

Deborah eased back in her chair and glanced at Brian's hand. She asked, "Do you have a family back in Boston or someone special?"

"Not really. I'm in between relationships," he said evasively, avoiding any gender pronouns. Instantly, he wished he had left his relationship status more ambiguous, realizing that Deborah might be looking for some fun while on holiday.

"So, you just came all by yourself?" she asked, gazing into his eyes. She was trying to get a read. Was he a gay man on a fantasy holiday to Morocco or a scientist from Boston ready to sell secrets to the Saudis? Or could he be both?

Brian nodded nervously. He then added, "So, you think Pierre could introduce me to some people at the University of Mohammed V? That would be outstanding."

"I'll ask. Are you here for a few days?"

"Yes. Here's my number," he said as he jotted his number on a small card.

She looked at it, looked at Brian, and said, "We'll be in touch. In the meantime, I think I better go check on Pierre."

"It was a pleasure."

"Mine, too," she said with a warm smile. "*À bientôt.*"

"*À bientôt.*"

12

Chapter Twelve – The First Sighting

The next day, after an early swim in the pool and a light breakfast, Brian went to the university. He hoped to get a formal introduction to Hadi through Pierre but, in the meantime, there was no reason not to be proactive and see if he could make a connection himself. He brought a book, sat on a bench across from the entrance to Hadi's building, and began to read. Around 10:30, to his surprise, he saw Omar walk out of the building surrounded by three men, all dressed in tailored jackets and dress pants. They were talking earnestly. He shook hands with the older man, and the other two escorted him down the steps and onto a walkway heading toward another cluster of buildings.

Brian had rehearsed in his head countless times what he would do if he spotted Omar, but he hadn't expected a grouping of what he presumed were university professors and administrators. Now was not the time to surprise Omar, so he pretended to read and, when they were far enough away, trailed them, concealing himself amongst the throng of students heading to classes.

Omar was intensively conversing with one of the two men, gesturing with his hands to make points. He nodded several times and seemed pensive. One of the two excused himself, shook Omar's hand, and walked away, entering a nearby building. Omar and the other man, somewhat younger and definitely the more handsome of the three, continued to walk along the sidewalk. They came to a road, and the man glanced at his phone. A few moments later, a black Mercedes pulled up, and the two got into the back seat of the car and sped off.

"Shit," Brian exclaimed. "What do I do now?" he asked himself out loud.

He looked up and down the walkway. Whatever was going on, Omar wasn't here to run away from his family. He looked like he was running toward something, something that seemed organized at top levels of the university or even the government. He was perturbed that Professor Hadi had been dishonest earlier and decided to confront him. He returned to his office, knocked, and heard an older voice say, "*Entrez.*"

Brian opened the door, and the elderly professor rose from his desk with a surprised look.

"*Je suis Brian, l'ami de Omar. On s'est parlé hier.*"

Aman cleared his throat and adjusted his tie, gazing intently at Brian. His outdated blue suit had become bulky as Aman had lost muscle and height over the years. Sweat formed on his furrowed forehead. He wasn't pleased with the intrusion, looked at his watch, and said, "I have to be at a meeting shortly. What can I do for you?"

"I'm concerned about my friend, and I need some information."

"I don't know what you are talking about," Aman said, repeating the line he used on the phone the day before.

"I saw you shake hands with Omar a short while ago. I know you know who he is."

Aman looked irritated but gestured toward one of the large chairs in front of his desk and said, "*Asseyez- vous.*"

In front of Aman's large oak desk were two upholstered chairs, a brass table, and a large, dark red Persian carpet. A wall of windows let in bright sunlight, and wooden bookcases lined the side walls. Aman walked around his desk and sat next to Brian.

"Who are you?" Aman began.

"I'm Brian LeBlanc. I'm a research scientist in Boston and a friend of Omar's."

Aman creased his forehead and wrung his hands. He seemed perplexed. He sat forward in his chair and said, "I'm surprised you are so bold in coming here."

"I was concerned about Omar. He left Boston abruptly."

"Maybe he wasn't interested."

Brian glanced across the room and then back at Aman. "So, he told you about us?"

"Yes."

"And?"

"I think he has a better offer here."

Brian creased his forehead. He thought back at the two men escorting Omar away from Aman's building and the one he entered the Mercedes with. He was definitely handsome and well-dressed. Maybe he had miscalculated Omar. Perhaps Omar was more experienced with men than he had let on. Maybe someone had been courting him from Morocco.

"I just want to make sure he's okay."

"Why would you think he's not?"

"We had a nice dinner in Boston. He left abruptly, and his family hasn't seen or heard from him."

"It was urgent that he come to Rabat right away and discretely."

"Who are you? And who are the men that were with him this morning?"

Aman pulled a handkerchief out of his pocket and wiped his forehead. He leaned on one of the arms of the large chair he sat in and said defiantly, "I'm not sure I have any obligation to divulge that information to you."

"Obviously, you don't. But, for Omar's sake, it would be helpful."

"Omar can decide for himself."

"I already know you are a physics professor and a Sufi shaykh."

Aman nodded and grinned.

"Who are the other two men?"

Aman looked over toward the bookcases pensively. He turned back toward Brian and said, "That's really not so confidential. If you must know, one is the dean of sciences, and the other is a member of the Royal Family."

"The tall, handsome one?"

Aman nodded.

"Is Omar involved with the Royal Family?" Brian asked, now worried this little escapade was a lot more complicated than he had imagined.

"Oh, my dear, no. What gave you that impression?"

"They seemed very friendly."

"They are doing what they can to solidify relations."

"I thought you just said he wasn't involved."

"Business relations."

"What?"

Aman was getting irritated and impatient. He stood up and paced. He then said emphatically, "Our offer is best for Omar."

"What offer?"

Aman was hesitant to respond but then said, "Oh well, what does it matter? You already know. We're trying to recruit him, as are you."

"For what?"

"The government needs high-level scientists to advance its technological agenda. As you undoubtedly know, Omar is brilliant. He speaks French and Arabic. He's the perfect candidate, someone who can facilitate Canadian and Moroccan collaboration as well."

What Aman didn't disclose were the deep pockets of the Saudis who hoped to get a leg up on new quantum technology. Morocco was a front for a more ambitious agenda. They wanted to keep the extent of things secret from the Americans and Europeans.

"Oh," Brian said, sighing deeply. "And I guess you think I'm someone trying to recruit him for Boston, for MIT?"

"Isn't that the case?"

"No, although now that you bring it up, it's not a bad idea. In fact, I came for personal reasons. Omar and I just became acquainted, and things seemed to have ended abruptly and without explanation."

"Ah," Aman said, rubbing his chin. "*Je vois maintenant.*"

Aman scrutinized Brian up and down. He raised his brows, as if recognizing something for the first time. He then added, "This represents a little wrinkle."

Brian felt warm and clammy, realizing that perhaps he had just outed Omar inadvertently.

"How do you know Omar?" Aman pressed, staring at Brian.

"We met unexpectedly when I had an accident in Quebec. His family repaired my car, and Omar brought it to me. We have mutual interests," Brian noted, hoping to spin his and Omar's emerging relationship in more professional terms. "He's a scientist and I'm a researcher in Boston."

Aman sighed but was still on alert.

"And you came to Morocco to find him?" Aman inquired further; his brow furrowed.

Brian nodded. "His family contacted me, concerned about his disappearance."

Aman stared at Brian, not sure what to think. "Let me speak with Omar later, and I'll relay that you are here on behalf of his family. You gave me your number the other day."

Brian nodded. "I would be very grateful."

"Well, I have an appointment," Aman said, extending his hand to Brian.

"Thank you for your time and thank you in advance for letting Omar know I am here."

Brian left Aman's office and headed to the main road near the campus to see if he might find a taxi. He hailed one from the curb and was quickly taken to the Sofitel.

Once inside his room, he sent a text to Hakim: "Hakim. Omar is in Rabat. From what I can tell, the government is trying to recruit him for work. It must have been secret, thus his abrupt and incommunicative departure."

Hakim responded: "That's great news. Have you spoken with him?"

"Not yet. I hope soon. I'll let you know what transpires."

Later that afternoon, Omar sat across from Aman in his office. Aman was nervous, one leg shaking and his eyes darting about the room.

"Your friend Brian showed up."

"What? Brian's here?"

"Yes. Apparently, your family was worried, tracked you down, and sent him to retrieve you."

"Wow! How did they find me?"

"I have no idea. Perhaps someone was able to get into your account and noticed the purchase for the flight. I knew we should have paid on our end."

"How can I get in touch with him? As instructed, I haven't turned on my phone."

"He's at the Sofitel."

"Is it okay for me to see him?"

Aman looked across the room as if in thought. He cleared his throat and said, "I think this might pose an issue."

"Why?" Omar asked, fearful that Aman might accuse him of being gay.

"There are a few things troubling me," Aman began.

Omar shuffled nervously in his seat.

"For one thing, he's a scientist in Boston. If government officials find out, and something goes wrong with our plans, they will have my head. You know how secret this new venture is."

"He's not here to recruit me. He's a graduate of MIT and works with them in biomedical research, but not in physics or quantum technology."

"Then why is he here?" Aman asked, leaning forward and staring at Omar sternly. "How well do you know him? Maybe he's been playing you all along."

"I don't know why he is here. My uncle must have reached out to him. They met recently during a snowstorm in Quebec."

Aman didn't look convinced. "You're telling me your uncle contacted a stranger to find you?"

"I know. It doesn't sound very convincing, but it's true."

"Why him and not your uncle or your father?"

Omar didn't know how to answer the question. He wracked his brain for a credible pretext.

"We were having dinner, and Brian thought I got in an accident on my way home."

"Yes, he mentioned that. But why would he come and not someone from your family?"

"I don't know. If I could talk with him, I could find out. Maybe he was coming here anyway or had a trip to Europe planned or something. I just don't know."

"I think you do," Aman said pointedly, hoping Omar would crack under pressure.

"No. I don't," Omar said emphatically and convincingly.

"You know it's *haram*," Aman said sternly.

Omar's heart raced nervously. The opportunity to lead an initiative between Morocco and Quebec on quantum technology was a dream come true. He felt the opportunity was now slipping through his fingers as he watched Aman crease his forehead.

He pulled himself together and defiantly asked, "What?"

"I think you know what. Unnatural relations. They are forbidden."

"I have been brought up a devout Muslim. I assure you; Brian and I are only acquaintances," Omar explained, now feeling himself sweat under Aman's scrutiny.

Aman still wasn't convinced. "So, do you have a fiancé?"

At least Omar could answer truthfully that he did. His family had been trying to arrange a marriage for years. "Yes. I do."

"When do you plan to marry?"

"After I get settled here."

Aman sighed and a timid smile crossed his face, although he still wasn't convinced Omar was being forthcoming.

"So, can I see him?" Omar pressed.

"I'm not sure. I would hate for Boston to find out about our project inadvertently. Even if Brian isn't here on behalf of MIT, he might know people and inadvertently disclose information."

"He doesn't have to know about the job," Omar assured him.

"He already does. We spoke. What do you think he thought when he saw us coming out of the building yesterday - that you picked up and flew to Morocco on a whim? However, he doesn't know the extent of the project nor its financing."

Aman scratched his head, looked out the window, and then said,

"Why don't you meet with him? Tell him the truth – that you're here for a job interview. Tell him it is confidential. Then send him on his way."

Omar nodded reluctantly.

Aman stood, extended his hand, and said, "Let's meet tomorrow after you see him. I hope we can finalize everything."

"Me, too. I'm looking forward to this opportunity.

13

Chapter Thirteen - The
Government

Later that afternoon, Aman met with the minister of science to sort things out.

"Thank you, Murad, for meeting. There seems to be a wrinkle in our plans with Omar," Aman began.

"I know. It would seem the Americans want to intercept him."

"What?"

"Brian LeBlanc is here on behalf of MIT and the Americans."

"He said he's here for personal reasons, on an errand for Omar's family."

"That's not what our sources picked up. This Brian is very well-versed in quantum physics and is interested in the intersection of quantum mechanics and biochemistry."

Aman scratched his head. "Really? Are you sure? He came across sincere to me – that he was here just to make sure Omar was okay. What I'm concerned about is that Omar might be gay." Then Aman scratched his chin and looked off pensively. "Now, perhaps even worse – Omar might be gay, and Brian might be an agent that is playing him."

"Did Omar come out to you?" Murad pressed; his eyes widened in alarm.

"No. In fact, he says he has a fiancé. But I'm not convinced. I think there's something between Brian and him."

"That's not such a problem. The more serious problem would be the Americans finding out what we are up to and dissuading Omar from coming here."

Aman paced back and forth in front of the windows, glancing out on the campus. He realized he might have given too much information about their research project to Brian, and he decided to focus more on the problem of Omar's possible sexual orientation. "How would it look if the press got wind that our new scientist from Quebec was gay? Or that the Saudis or other potential financial partners found that out as well?"

"The world is changing, Aman. He's from Quebec, a liberal country where gay marriage exists. It might actually make us look good, that we are open to diversity and can recruit the best talent from anywhere in the world. The Saudis can also wave it off as a problem in Morocco, not in their own backyard."

Aman turned red and perspired. "It's a little more complicated than that," he said, clearing his throat.

Murad leaned forward, encouraging Aman to continue.

"Thirty-five years ago, Omar's uncle, Nassen, stumbled upon his father, Khalid, having sex with a senior government official. Nassen was 10. He was young enough to be startled and confused by what he saw. The government official was fearful the talkative little boy might say something inadvertently. There were enough rumors as it was, so corroborating testimony would have ended his career. He gave Khalid and his family a generous gift to leave the country and immigrate to Canada, where they promptly started a business."

"Wow, what an interesting story. It's ironic Omar is back here. But I don't see why that complicates things."

"If Omar is openly gay, and news got out, the press might insinuate that you or me or this government official – who will remain unnamed – recruited him for other reasons – to keep his family quiet or, even worse, to court Omar. That could sabotage collaboratives. I can't put my reputation at risk as a professor and Sufi Shaykh, nor do I presume you want to place your job at risk."

Murad could see the perspiration on Aman's forehead and wondered if there wasn't more to the story that involved Aman. "Why don't we talk to Omar, get it out in the open, and see if it will be a problem? Maybe he's not gay."

Aman took a deep breath and said, "I think we should go with our second choice for the job, Philippe. He speaks French, he's half-Moroccan, he's brilliant, and there's no risk."

"But he is from France, not Canada. He doesn't give us the leverage we wanted with Quebec and its initiatives in quantum computing technology, and he's not as talented as Omar," Murad added.

"I know, but as a French speaker, we can get him a working visa for Canada, and we'll be okay. And it keeps the Americans off our backs."

"But Omar is the more natural choice and is exceptionally talented," Murad pleaded.

"Too much risk," Aman said matter-of-factly.

"I still say we talk with Omar. What do we have to lose? If he's too much of a gamble, then we can go forward with Philippe. But if he checks out okay, then we have an ideal candidate."

Aman nodded reluctantly.

A while later, Aman called Omar. "I met with Murad. We would like to have another interview with you. Are you free tomorrow morning?"

"Sure. Where and what time?"

"My office at 9. By the way, did you line up an appointment with Brian?"

"Not yet. We haven't connected. I was thinking dinner this evening if I can reach him."

Aman thought a moment and then smiled to himself. "Sure. Why don't you call him at the Sofitel and have dinner or a drink with him there? This will assuage his and your family's concerns."

"*D'accord. Merci, Aman.*"

"*De rien.* I hope this settles matters."

Omar hung up the phone, surprised by Aman's change of demeanor and eagerness for him to meet Brian. He wondered what was up.

After speaking with Omar, Aman called Murad.

"Murad. I have an idea. Omar is going to meet with Brian at the Sofitel this evening. Can you send some of your men there to do some reconnaissance, perhaps some remote listening? This way, we can be sure about Omar and about Brian as well."

"I'll send a team right away. I know the perfect pair."

Omar called the Sofitel and was connected to Brian's room. Unexpectedly, Brian picked up the phone. "*Allô.*"

"*Brian. C'est Omar.*"

There was a long pause on the other end of the line before Brian said, "*Omar. Qu'est-ce qui se passe?* What happened?"

Omar didn't answer Brian's question. He just said, "Brian. It's good to hear your voice."

Brian noted Omar's lack of enthusiasm or elaboration. He didn't respond right away, realizing that perhaps the phone was bugged, and Omar was being cautious.

"Can we meet later?" Omar inquired. "It would be good to visit."

Omar didn't share pleasantries or even attempt to explain why he was in Rabat.

"Dinner here at the hotel?" Brian offered, without pressing Omar for more information.

"Does seven sound good?"

"*Parfait*," Brian responded.

"*À bientôt.*" Omar concluded.

At seven, Omar arrived in a taxi at the front of the hotel and was directed to the restaurant. The maître d' pointed to a table where Brian was already seated and having a drink.

As Brian looked up at Omar approaching, he felt his heart pound and his legs grow weak. Omar walked confidently forward in a casual pair of slacks, a light cotton dress shirt, and a tailored suit jacket. It seemed odd to see Omar in summer clothes. His skin was radiant and his dark brows and lashes more alluring than ever.

Brian gripped the arm of his chair, restraining his urge to leap up and give Omar a warm embrace and moist kiss. He suspected they were being watched - that Aman wanted to make sure Omar was a safe wager, that nothing nefarious was going on between them and that Brian indeed was not a recruiting agent for the Americans.

Omar was excited to see Brian but was on alert as well, concealing his affection. Brian stood and stoically embraced Omar, who responded warmly but guardedly. Their gazes lingered as they took seats opposite each other.

Brian looked nervously around the room. Many tables were foursomes, married couples meeting friends for dinner, a birthday, or a celebration of some sort. One or two tables were occupied by single men who looked like they were in town for business or political affairs. Near to their table were two men having cocktails and appetizers. Brian had spotted them earlier. They looked like they could be businessmen, but their shoes were just not up to par with men traveling to Morocco to seal corporate deals, and their ties were out-of-date. Brian wondered if they might not be two lovers meeting under the pretext of a business meeting, but here again, they failed the test. Their hair cuts were conservative, their gestures unrefined, and there was no spark or passion in their eyes or in their body language.

Brian had read enough spy thrillers to know that it was easy to set up a temporary listening device in a setting like the restaurant. He slipped a piece of paper out of the pocket of his jacket and wrote a quick note to Omar, sliding it toward him as if he were reaching for his glass of water. "I think we are being watched and listened to. Be on best behavior."

Omar nodded and said, "I'm glad we could meet."

"Me, too. I bring greetings from your uncles."

"I realize they must have been worried by my departure."

Brian nodded.

"I received an urgent call to come for a job interview."

"What kind of job?"

"Oh, nothing very impressive. It's a university position," he said, downplaying its significance.

"Well, that sounds impressive to me. And in Morocco, of all places!"

"Well, yes. That is a bit ironic, isn't it?" Omar replied.

"You must be excited."

Omar nodded, trying to conceal a smile. "And Tariq and Hassan?" he asked, shifting attention away from the job opportunity.

"Hakim has been taking good care of them," Brian said, raising one of his brows.

Omar felt himself turn red with embarrassment. He dreaded having to face his family and only hoped a lucrative job offer in Rabat would minimize their expected displeasure and interrogation. He fidgeted with his napkin, not sure what to say next. He felt his pulse race as Brian smiled warmly across the table. A few days ago, the trip to Rabat seemed to have made sense, to have been a promising opportunity. Now this affable and endearing man sitting across from him was a reminder of all he would likely have to give up, and he now had second thoughts.

Brian sensed Omar's distress and broke the awkward silence with something he hoped Omar would find easy to talk about. "So why did you specialize in theoretical physics? It is a rare and unusual field of study."

Omar smiled. He appreciated Brian's professional discretion and relished the opportunity to talk about his passion.

"At the mosque, we learned that many of the most innovative scientists in the Middle Ages were Muslim. Islam preserved the great philosophical texts of ancient Greece and integrated them with mathematics, astronomy, and physics. I had always been embarrassed growing up Muslim in a predominantly Catholic country. My classmates perceived us as backward, uneducated, and conservative. One day I woke up and said, 'I'll show them! I'm going to be a cutting-edge scientist. People will once again see Muslims as enlightened.' The next day I began filling out an application for Laval University."

Brian observed Omar's youthful excitement, the gleam in his eyes, his expressive gestures, and his body taut with passion and energy. He felt himself stiffen with arousal, remembering their time in bed, the softness of his skin and its distinctive aroma and heat. He heard Omar, but wasn't paying attention to the words. Instead, he was scrutinizing the stunning man before him. He reached for his glass of wine and had to restrain himself from reaching beyond the glass to graze Omar's hand.

There was an awkward pause as Brian realized he had missed much of what Omar had recounted. He struggled to latch onto a line of thought and asked, "Did you know you wanted to go into physics? Why not medicine or the environment?"

"I was fortunate to have a great physics teacher in high school. I was struck by innovative paradigms that were being considered in the light of recent research. It felt like physics would be the field most likely to change our whole sense of the world, of the universe. I thought to myself, 'If you want to make your mark, theoretical physics will be the place.'"

"But even the greatest geniuses haven't been able to make sense of quantum physics and how the quantum level and the world we observe interface," Brian pointed out.

Omar leaned forward, his elbows on the table, and his eyes staring into Brian's. "I know. Isn't that exciting? No one has solved it yet. It just takes imagination."

Brian forced a smile, realizing Omar was diving in headfirst, ready to take the scientific world by storm. There was chemistry between them, and longing in Omar's eyes as he gazed into Brian's, but there was no doubt Omar was moving to Morocco and leaving his gay self behind.

Omar noticed the twitch on Brian's left cheek. The glimmer in his eyes had dimmed, and Brian looked evasively down at his glass of wine. He fussed with his fork and ran his fingers over the menu.

Brian glanced over at the two men nearby. They had finally ordered a charcuterie plate. They seem bored, increasingly convinced Omar and Brian were certifiable academic nerds.

"Shall we order?" Brian asked.

Omar nodded. The server came to the table, took their orders, and retreated to the kitchen. As they waited for their meals to arrive, Omar broke the heavy silence.

"And you. Why biomedical research?"

"For the same reasons, although less religious. After the estrangement from my parents, I wanted to show them and others that I could overcome any obstacle and be successful. My parents had several friends who were medical doctors and swooned over them at dinner and other social occasions. I guess unconsciously, I was trying to regain their esteem."

"Or perhaps get revenge?" Omar suggested with a chuckle.

"Maybe both. I was also impressed with what I perceived to be the magic of medicine – the ability to change the course of evil, of sickness, of disease and restore someone to health."

"Then you went into research, right?"

"Yes. I realized there was a lot of money in it, and Boston was the epicenter of the industry. I liked the city and wanted to stay. A lucrative company recruited me, and I have never looked back."

Omar raised his glass of wine to take a sip. His eyes floated over the rim of the glass. His eyes said, 'We're cut from the same cloth, both wanting to prove something, to overcome the stigmas that mire us. I admire you. I get you. You get me.' He wondered if their affection was more collegial than sexual. At least if that was the case, his decision to move to Morocco would be less painful.

Omar followed Brian's eyes to the nearby table. They both raised their brows. One of the two men rose and walked to the bar while the other remained, checking messages and emails on his phone. Brian glanced toward the bar and recognized Deborah. Pierre was with her. The man who had been at the table in the dining room slid up next to them casually. He pretended to check his phone while taking long sips of wine. Pierre pivoted and faced the dining room while Deborah took a long sip of wine and said a few words to him. He nodded, placed his empty glass on the bar and returned to the table and his companion. Brian wondered if Deborah and Pierre knew the men and, if so, were Pierre and Deborah really just French tourists?

A few moments later, a server brought the agents their main courses, a mixture of lamb, olives, and other spices served on a bed of rice. One of them seemed interested in talking. The other was annoyed and seemed eager for their assignment to be over. He leaned toward his companion and made several gestures. Brian thought they were desperate and impatient pleas to wrap the operation up.

The other one glanced toward Omar and Brian. Brian caught his eye and nodded. The agent nodded back and then turned to his partner. They quickly finished their meal, paid their tab, and left.

Omar slid a piece of paper toward Brian. "Don't fall for their ploy."

Brian shook his head, realizing the listening device might still be active or, worse, they had somehow managed to infiltrate his phone through the Wi-Fi system. He would do a security scan later.

Their meals arrived, and they both were relieved to focus on something practical. As they began to eat, Brian slipped in a difficult question. "When do you go back to Quebec?"

Omar flinched, not sure if he should divulge the timetable.

"Sorry. I didn't mean to pry," Brian interjected. "I'm sure you have a lot to do before you return home."

Omar nodded. "Will you let my family know everything is good here? They'll be happy to know the investment they made in my education will pay off."

"What will they think about you returning to Morocco?" Brian asked, wondering if the reason for his family's departure would leave them feeling ambivalent about Omar moving back.

Omar sensed Brian's deeper curiosity but couldn't elaborate. "They will be happy that I have reconnected with my heritage and relieved that I will pursue science in the context of our religion."

As they ate, they chatted about Rabat, about its history, culture, and geography. Brian was annoyed at the superficiality of their exchanged and decided to move things in a more serious direction. "I'm curious. How does a Muslim integrate science with religion? I realize it happened in one age, but it seems less likely today."

"That's part of the challenge that excites me," Omar said, his eyes widening with enthusiasm.

Brian gave Omar a look of encouragement. "Continue."

"During the height of Islamic civilization, one that included Morocco and Andalusia, there were Sufi philosophers who elaborated theories about *tawhid* and reason. One of them I've followed closely was Ibn Al' Arabi. *Tawhid* refers to the unity of Allah – the oneness of Allah. The scholars argued that if God is one, then what God creates and what God reveals must be consistent. The world or the universe is a reflection of God. In fact, it is the imagination of God. To assist humans, God also reveals Godself in the form of revelation, prophets, and scripture – the Qur'an, for example."

"So, what does that have to do with science?"

"If science is the activity of knowing the world, studying what God has created, then how can it be any less important than theology and the study of scripture? Both study what God says or reveals — one in a text; the other in the world, no less a reflection of God's mind than the Qur'an."

"Most scientists today are not very religious. Religion has been cruel to us."

"Admittedly," Omar replied and nodded. "That's why I'm even more eager to do this. We need to change the relationship between science and religion. It will be good for religion. It will catapult religion forward, earning it respect once again."

"That's only if religion can embrace what you uncover."

"It must, or it is no longer relevant."

"Isn't that the direction we're headed?"

"Yes, but it's not inevitable. And I think theoretical physics is the most interesting area of synergy. There are so many interesting phenomena being discovered, such as entanglement and nonlocality, the primacy of consciousness over matter, and holographic models of storing information as wave interference patterns, patterns that have been enfolded over eons. All of the universe is present to us at the quantum level."

Brian smiled in astonishment. "I had no idea."

"Bet you thought I was a backwater Arab from Sherbrooke."

"Definitely not. That was never my impression."

Omar blushed. He was grateful that the two agents were probably only listening and that they couldn't see his delight in Brian.

"Back to your returning to Morocco – why not someplace like Boston?" As Brian asked the question, he noticed the agents glancing toward them.

"The science-religion opportunity is greater here – and important to me," Omar answered.

Brian closed his eyes in disappointment. Omar took a deep breath. Brian's disappointment was palpable. Omar tried to interject some humor and asked, "Have you been skiing again? I miss my coach."

Brian smiled and shook his head no, relieved at the reprieve. He played along for the sake of the agents. "Do you think he might be available for more lessons? I assume you enjoyed learning."

"It was more than I had expected. Thrilling and challenging at the same time."

"You seemed like a natural. There wasn't much of a learning curve, I hear."

Omar blushed. He then said playfully, "I'm ready to take on the steeper runs. From what I understand, the way to tackle them is head on, leaning down the mountain, straight on, straight ahead."

"No hesitation is key."

"Yes. I've heard that."

They chuckled at the exchange. But their laughter couldn't mask the undercurrent of remorse both felt. Could this be the end of the road? They finished their meals, paid the tab, and walked to the front of the hotel. The two men seated near them earlier were at the bar, talking with another man, and glancing down at their phones, presumably transcriptions of the conversation.

Omar shook Brian's hand firmly and slipped a piece of paper into Brian's palm. Brian glanced up, seeking some clue or signal. Omar gave him none, nodding instead at the attendant to wave down a taxi.

A car pulled up, and Omar stepped in, giving Brian a perfunctory wave. The car sped off, and Brian stood at the curb, wondering what might be next. He walked back into the hotel and glanced down at the piece of paper Omar slipped him.

"Pick me up in a rental car tomorrow at 11 AM in front of the Botanical Gardens."

14

Chapter Fourteen – Crossroads

Brian approached the concierge desk.

"*Est-ce que je peux vous aider?*" the attendant asked.

"*Oui.* I need a rental car for tomorrow. Can I arrange it with you?"

"Certainly. How long do you need it? Type of car?"

"Just one day. A regular sedan will do. Perhaps tomorrow morning around 10 AM?"

"Name?"

"*Monsieur LeBlanc, chambre 401.*"

"*Parfait.* It will be out front tomorrow morning. *Autre chose?*"

"Nothing else. I appreciate your help."

Brian pivoted from the concierge desk and headed toward the bar. He noticed Deborah and Pierre and approached them.

"Brian," Deborah exclaimed. They exchanged kisses on their cheeks, and Brian extended his hand to Pierre.

"Brian," he said, introducing himself.

"Pierre," he said in return. "*Enchanté.* Deborah mentioned you are from Boston and do research there."

Brian nodded, not really interested in a protracted conversation about science.

"Was that a colleague of yours earlier?" Pierre inquired.

Brian wasn't sure how to answer. "An acquaintance from Canada."

"Ah. And how is it you ended up here in Morocco at the same time? Deborah mentioned you were here on a respite from the cold."

"It was a coincidence. We bumped into each other unexpectedly," Brian lied.

"What does your colleague do?" Deborah asked, pressing for confirming information.

"Oh, he's a scientist, too. He's here on an academic exchange."

"That's interesting," Pierre said. "Who is he working with? I know a few people at the university here."

"Yes, Deborah mentioned that."

Brian wanted to respect Omar's privacy and the delicate nature of his job interview and said, "I'm not really sure."

"I have some friends in the science department at the University of Mohammed V," Pierre led.

"Who?"

"You probably wouldn't know them. They are teaching assistants, trying to get their foot in the door. They all work with an older guy, someone named Aman Hadi," Pierre said.

Brian tried to conceal his surprise at Hadi's name. He evasively looked to the barman to ask for a drink and then, once composed, turned to Pierre. "I have heard of him. What is his expertise?"

"I think it's physics or something like that."

"That's curious. That's an interest of mine, although not my field."

"Well, if you need introductions, let me know."

Brian nodded.

"So, Brian, any plans for touring?" Deborah asked.

Brian took a long sip of his drink and said, "I might take a drive tomorrow – see some historic sites here and there."

"Anything in particular?"

"Meknes, or perhaps places along the south coast. I've heard Essouira is nice, but it seems like a long drive."

"Hmm," Deborah murmured. "Yes. Places along the south coast are fascinating and beautiful, although it is still a little chilly for the beaches."

The three of them chatted. Deborah kept the conversation superficial, touristy. Pierre swooped in from time to time with a question about research, science, and Boston to see if Brian might slip and say something inadvertently. They were both still concerned Brian might be peddling sensitive research to the Saudis via Morocco.

Around 10, Brian excused himself and headed to his room. He checked emails, washed up, and went to bed. He was restless, turning this way and that, trying to find a comfortable position. The dinner with Omar had been both enchanting and disturbing. He was deeply drawn to Omar, spellbound by his alluring eyes, radiant caramel skin, and dark hair. Omar's rushed trip to Morocco and evasiveness around the job opportunity created a certain mystique that held Brian's interest, something he wasn't used to with casual relationships. Now the invitation for a clandestine getaway only added to the intrigue.

Brian's rule of thumb was to remain unentangled – to keep things brief and tidy. He had a nice romp with Omar in Quebec, had assuaged his conscience in finding him safe in Rabat, and could now move on to other pastures. He wondered why he was having difficulty letting go. He continued to toss and turn and finally fell to sleep.

He rose the next morning, had a nice breakfast, and then returned to his room to dress. He had no idea where Omar wanted to go, so he dressed in jeans, a shirt, and a light sweater. He packed a few other items – a swimsuit, some shorts, and a nicer jacket in case a dinner out was on the agenda.

At 10, he went downstairs and met the concierge who had him sign papers for his rental and handed him the keys. "Do you need a map?" the agent asked.

"No. I'll use GPS," Brian replied. "Although, if you can point me toward the Botanical Gardens, I would be grateful."

The agent looked up nervously at a couple of men standing off to the side. He glanced back at Brian and explained how best to get to the Gardens. As he did, the two men got into their car and waited for Brian.

"Thanks. That all makes sense."

Brian got into the car and sped off. The agent texted Brian's destination to the agents.

Brian turned onto the main boulevard in front of the hotel and then pulled over. He decided using GPS would be better, given his unfamiliarity with the roadways. He typed in the address and heard a silky French male voice give directions.

The route took him through the university section of the city, one that he was all too familiar with already. He took his time, taking in the scenery now that he was more relaxed. The university was set in a nice section of the city, with broad expanses of parkland, terraces, walkways, and modern classroom buildings. Even though the university was impressive, he wondered how someone like Omar would choose a place like Rabat over Quebec City or Boston or any other number of places that might be interested in recruiting him. He respected Omar's interest in making a difference in Islam but couldn't imagine Rabat holding his attention for long.

Eventually, the GPS voice directed him to a boulevard that bordered the Botanical Gardens. Given Rabat's semi-arid weather, the gardens had more of a Mediterranean look than something one might find in northern Europe. The gardens showcased majestic junipers, cedars, and pines – all with gnarly trunks diving deep into the dry soil for water. There were garden beds filled with pomegranate bushes and other flowering tropical plants. Brian slowed, searching for Omar.

Omar sauntered out from a small cluster of trees and glanced at the road, noticing Brian's slowly moving sedan. He waved, and Brian stopped, opening the door for him. Omar hopped into the passenger seat.

Both stared at each other intensely. Omar's skin was aglow. A subtle fragrance of verbena and rosemary emanated from his neck. Brian thought the aroma must be from a distinctive blend of soap used locally. He had on a short-sleeve blue polo shirt and light cotton shorts and colorful tennis shoes. Brian couldn't take his eyes off Omar's dark, hairy legs, shaking nervously.

Omar breathed in Brian's cologne and felt the heat of his body only inches from him. He was tempted to lean over and give him a kiss, but knew that would be a risky move. He hoped Brian sensed the yearning in his eyes.

After what seemed like an interminable pause, Brian asked, "Where to?"

"Why don't you drive forward? If you are up for it, I thought we might go to Volubilis, an ancient Roman city and archaeological site. It's out of the city and not a place where we are likely to run into people. It's only a couple of hours away."

"Sounds good to me," Brian said stoically, still uncertain of how things might unfold. "Why don't you type in the site in your GPS?"

"I still have my phone switched off. Can we use yours?"

Brian nodded and handed his phone to Omar. Omar typed in the site's name and the silky French male voice gave instructions. The GPS directed them to head forward and then make a left turn in about 500 meters. The route took them back past the Sofitel and then along the edge of the university. "I feel like I've made this trek before," Brian said humorously, raising his eyebrows.

Omar just nodded, his legs continuing to shake nervously.

Brian glanced down and asked, "What's up? You seem tense."

"It's nothing. It's all surreal – sitting here with you and heading out to do sightseeing in Morocco."

"Hm. Yes. It is rather odd. Does Hadi know you're playing hooky?"

Omar blushed.

Brian added, "I take it he doesn't."

Omar shook his head. He was supposed to be making arrangements for his move to Rabat. He had accepted the position, but didn't want to tell Brian yet. He wasn't sure why he was in the car with him. It seemed like a good idea the night before. Now it seemed disingenuous, unfair to Brian.

The voice on the GPS system guided them to a highway. They passed through a dusty suburban industrial district and then quickly into a forested area. The woods were a pleasant relief from the dryness around Rabat. From time to time, the road bordered farmland with rustic stands selling vegetables, fruit, and other products.

From the moment they left the city, Brian had noticed a dark Mercedes trailing them. He kept glancing in the rear-view mirror.

"You're not aware of any reason someone would be following us, do you?" Brian asked.

Omar turned around and noticed the car. He began to perspire. "No. No one should know where I am or who I am with. It's probably just someone heading out to their weekend villa or making the trip to Meknes. Or at least I hope so."

"Maybe we should pull off and get a snack at one of these stands. Maybe they will keep going," Brian said. Omar nodded enthusiastically.

A few moments later, Omar pointed to a tent on the right side of the road, and Brian pulled in quickly, a cloud of dust enveloping them as they slowed to a stop and parked the car. Brian opened his door and noticed the Mercedes continuing swiftly on the highway. Omar got out of his side of the car, and they walked toward the farm stand.

A peasant woman welcomed them first in Arabic and then in French. Omar spoke to her in Arabic and asked for some coffee and some cakes. She smiled, fixed them some coffee, and invited them to take a seat at the dusty table set under a faded umbrella.

"What do you think?" Omar asked awkwardly, trying to break the silence.

"You mean of this?" Brian asked as he waved his hand over the nearby terrain.

Omar nodded.

"I guess I didn't know what to expect. Desert, palm trees, and whitewashed medinas were the cliché images I had of Morocco. It's more modern and greener than I expected."

Omar smiled. He realized this would be his home. He took a deep breath and let the idea sink in. He quickly consumed the espresso and cake, and watched Brian finish his as well.

"Shall we?" Omar added, standing up and walking toward the car.

Both got in, took their seats, and then buckled up. As Omar latched his seat belt, he looked up into Brian's eyes, hovering inches from his. He wanted to lean forward and give him a kiss, but the proprietors of the roadside stand were cleaning their table, and he decided to hold back.

Brian turned on the motor and sped off onto the highway. He took a deep breath and said, "So, we're alone and without surveillance."

Omar looked nervously at Brian. He said, "I'm sorry for putting you through all of this. I appreciate the concern you had for me and the help you gave my family." Omar rubbed his left hand over Brian's thigh.

"I was worried."

"I can see why. I'm sorry about all the mystery."

"So, what will you do?"

It was the question Omar didn't want to answer. He knew he was taking the job and moving to Rabat, but he realized it meant concealing his sexuality and giving up the opportunity to have a relationship with someone like Brian. It seemed unimaginable, yet certain. "I'm not sure yet. I'm still trying to decide, to make sense of it all," he said disingenuously.

"Well, let's enjoy the day together," Brian suggested. "I enjoy being with you," Brian added, reaching over and taking hold of Omar's warm, soft hand.

Omar melted and felt himself become aroused, shifting in his seat. He looked over at Brian. He loved Brian's playfulness and affability, his dramatic gestures, his expressive eyes, and his quick wit. He was smart, yet unassuming. He stared at Brian's crotch and noticed it had firmed up. He wanted to reach over, unzip his pants, and reach inside for Brian's cock.

They continued to drive. Brian decided to be more forward and played with the tail of Omar's shirt, lifting it slightly and sliding his hand up under the fabric, feeling the warmth underneath. Omar smiled. He looked over his shoulder and, since there were no cars behind them, he ran his hand over Brian's shoulder, fingering the back of Brian's head and hair. Brian grinned, glancing back and forth between the road and Omar's face. He leaned over and gave Omar a quick kiss. "You have such killer eyes!" he whispered.

Omar felt his heart accelerate and his skin moisten with desire for Brian. "Do you want to skip Volubilis?" he asked hesitatingly.

"And do what?"

"I don't know. Perhaps a hike in the forest," he suggested with a grin.

Brian was tempted and paused in thought. Then he said, "All I need is for a Moroccan farmer or hunter to find us, and we'd be toast. Let's stick to our plan. Maybe there are some hidden rooms in the old Roman villas." He winked at Omar.

Omar raised his eyebrow. He could feel his heart pound forcefully. He ran his fingers down the side of Brian's neck and loosened the top button of his shirt.

They continued the drive, both quiet, using their eyes and hands to communicate. They made their way around the outer neighborhoods of Meknes and headed toward the archaeological park.

"Are you hungry?" Brian asked.

Omar nodded. "I imagine there must be some kind of café at the archaeological site. Should we go there right away and check things out?"

"Sounds good," Brian said.

In a quarter of an hour, they noticed signs for the archaeological park and, to their delight, found an upscale café and restaurant at the edge of the grounds. It looked out over the olive groves nearby. Brian parked the car, and they went inside. The owners greeted Omar in Arabic and then shifted to French, handing Brian and Omar menus and showing them a nice table on the terrace.

The owners brought out tea, some hummus, and then a stew made of lamb and winter vegetables.

After lunch, they walked to the ruins and began their tour.

Brian had traveled extensively, and had visited great archaeological sites at Ephesus, Athens, Delphi, and Rome. He had seen the great temples in Sicily and extensive excavations at Pompeii and Ostia Antica. From the entrance of the park, the ruins looked important but not particularly impressive. A few columns and arches pierced the otherwise broad and flat landscape, with mountains rising in the distance. There were few tourists as it was off season.

They walked up the steps of the ancient Roman temple and through the soaring arched walls of the old basilica. What Brian hadn't expected were the extensive mosaics uncovered in the sumptuous villas that made up this prosperous Roman provincial city. Although somewhat faded in the African sun, the mosaics were still colorful and of great artistic quality and detail. Some mosaics were decorative geometric motifs, but others included detailed images of Greek and Roman gods and goddesses. Inside some of the excavated buildings, there were well-preserved remnants of olive presses, baths, and plumbing.

The sun was bright, and Brian savored the warmth on his face, neck, and forearms. Omar's hair glistened in the light, and his weepy dark brown eyes seemed particularly sexy as they strolled near each other through the various structures. From time to time, Brian let his hand graze Omar's. They both seemed eager to pounce on each other as they found themselves alone at the edge of the excavations.

"So, any more thoughts about the university position?" Brian interjected as they strolled through several of the more prominent villas.

Omar shook his head, unwilling to disclose the inevitable.

"Do you want to talk about it?" Brian inquired.

Omar stared into Brian's eyes with little emotion, then he said evasively, "You know, in Roman times, men married out of social obligation but enjoyed friendship with each other. Imagine the baths – handsome men lounging about in the nude, taking in the sun and the warm water."

Brian raised his eyebrows. He thought the segue odd. He realized the old Roman arrangement wasn't far off from what occurred in Morocco today and wondered if the remark was Omar's way of hinting at his plan for the future. Brian thought carefully and then replied, "It's interesting how marriage has evolved to be more love-based. Today, people marry out of love and expect their spouses to share emotional intimacy with them."

"Yes. I know," Omar noted without elaboration.

Brian wanted to make a point, to encourage Omar to embrace love rather than social duty or convention, but realized his own behavior was far from exemplary. He realized he had settled in his own way – a nice professional life coupled with fun sex on the side. He avoided all the commitment and complications of intimacy. All he could say was, "Maybe we aren't so different from the Romans after all."

Omar wondered if Brian had already guessed his choice. He still wasn't sure what he had hoped to accomplish by inviting Brian on an excursion. Was this a trial run for future clandestine relationships? Was this his future – a secretive, quick, and short rendezvous? His gut tightened at the thought of a blow job in the back of a car or something more involved behind a grove of trees. On the other hand, what did he owe Brian, a confirmed single gay guy who thrived on anonymous and recreational sex? Could he and Brian become fuck buddies who would meet up in Boston and Rabat from time to time under the pretext of research? Was that an acceptable compromise for them both?

He gazed at the back of Brian's head as he peered over a colorful mosaic. Brian seemed deep in thought and turned around, catching Omar's intense look. They both stood facing each other, struggling between reticence and longing. Omar glanced right and left, realizing they were alone and out-of-sight. He leaned over and gave Brian a deep, long kiss. Brian kissed him back, breathing Omar in and letting the wetness between them linger on his tongue. Omar traced his hand over the front of Brian's bulging jeans, feeling the hardness underneath.

Brian pulled back slightly and gave Omar a curious look. Omar smiled warmly, encouragingly. Brian leaned back casually over the mosaic and said, "You're one mysterious man, Omar Aziz."

"I'm sorry. I don't want to take advantage of you. I'm so conflicted." Omar began to tear up.

Brian turned around, faced Omar, and traced his finger over his eyes, rubbing out his tears. He ran his fingers over Omar's dark brows and said, "Those orbs!"

They gazed at each other for a few moments more and then Brian said, "Should we finish the tour?"

Omar couldn't speak, choked with emotion. He nodded.

They continued strolling through the excavations until they had exhausted the main part of the archaeological park. Brian looked at his watch and said, "We should head back to Rabat. Don't you have a flight tomorrow?"

Omar nodded. "I assume you're heading back, too?"

"Yes. I only managed to get a few days off. I have a big project due next week."

They got into the car and began the drive back to Rabat. Both were quiet, unsure where to take the conversation or their relationship. "Are you free for dinner?" Brian interjected as they got closer to the city.

"Unfortunately, I'm not. I have to meet with Hadi."

Brian felt his heart skip a beat. "Don't."

"What do you mean, don't? I have to meet with them. They are going to present their offer."

"I thought they already had," he said, sensing that Omar had already made his decision.

"No, they are still piecing it together," Omar replied, lying.

"What are you going to do?"

"I don't know," Omar replied again, lying.

Brian sensed Omar was not being entirely truthful or forthcoming, but didn't want to push or provoke him. He settled into a protracted silence.

Omar sensed Brian's sadness but didn't know how to alleviate it without being even more deceitful, so he remained quiet, too.

The ride back to Rabat seemed interminable with little more than superficial chit chat between them.

"Where do you want me to drop you?" Brian finally asked as they entered the outskirts of the city.

"The Botanical Gardens is good. I'm staying nearby."

"Do you want to meet up at the airport tomorrow?"

"I better not in case Hadi or others are there. They still think you are trying to recruit me."

"Are you sure?" Brian asked, sensing that Hadi's actual concern was whether Omar was gay or not.

Omar didn't respond.

A few moments later, Brian pulled up in front of the gardens. The evening light was brilliant – a warm, orange-yellow glow that was common along the coast. Brian shut the motor and got out. He walked around the car and gave Omar an embrace. He sensed Omar's tension and said, "No one should have a problem with a friendly embrace, right?"

Omar nodded.

"Let me know how things go," Brian added.

Omar extracted himself from Brian and walked along the path toward the other side of the park. Brian got back into the car and headed to the Sofitel where he greeted the same attendant from the morning, gave him the car keys, and thanked him for arranging the rental.

Brian began to tremble, adrenaline coursing through his body. He was angry at Omar, and he was angry at himself. How could someone so brilliant make such an irrational decision – a decision that refutes their authentic self? And how could he be falling for him? It made no sense.

Brian strolled into the bar area and noticed Deborah and Pierre. They were the last people he wanted to spend time with, but before he could turn around, they spotted him and waved. Reluctantly, he continued forward and said, "Well, fancy meeting the two of you. I thought you would be out to dinner or on an excursion."

"We had some appointments this afternoon, so we finished the day early. We didn't think you'd be back so soon. Weren't you heading south?"

"Change of plans. Back sooner than I expected," Brian said with little emotion. He waved the bartender down and asked for a glass of red wine, avoiding eye contact with Deborah and Pierre.

"When are you heading back to Boston? I can still make some introductions at the university," Pierre offered.

"Unfortunately, I have to head back tomorrow. My stay here was just a quick reprieve from winter. Back to reality."

"That's too bad," Deborah noted.

Brian was staring at his glass of wine. Deborah glanced over at Pierre, who nodded. Pierre cleared his throat and began, "Brian, how was Volubilis?"

Brian looked up, raised his eyebrow, and said, "What?"

"How was your visit to the archaeological site?"

"Were you there?" Brian inquired, wondering if, by some odd chance of fate, they had ended up at the same destination and, if so, had they seen him and Omar?

"No, but our colleagues were."

Brian looked inquisitively at Deborah, who gave him an apologetic smile. She then glanced at Pierre.

"Brian, let's cut to the chase," Pierre said more emphatically. "Deborah and I work for the US government."

Brian's eyes widened, and he took a long sip of his wine.

Deborah continued, "What Pierre wants to say is that we monitor research scientists who the government suspects might be peddling sensitive research information to other entities, particularly the Saudis, via unassuming contacts in places like Morocco."

"You're kidding!"

"No. We're not." Deborah pulled a badge out of her purse and flashed it at Brian discreetly.

"So, what does this have to do with me?"

"Well, you're a research scientist from Boston traveling to Morocco – alone. You had interests in academic contacts, including Omar. We had to follow through and check you out."

"I'm not sharing information with anyone."

"We know."

"So, why are we having this conversation?"

Deborah looked at Pierre, who then turned to Brian. "Well, we are always looking for people we might collaborate with."

"And?"

"Well, it would appear your colleague, Omar, is perhaps a bit more than a colleague you just ran into by chance."

"I don't know what you're talking about," Brian said emphatically.

"Would this help?" Pierre asked, holding up a photo on his phone to Brian.

Brian squinted at the photo and realized it was a shot of him and Omar kissing at Volubilis. He felt his heart skip a beat. "Someone was in the Mercedes, right?"

"Perhaps. But physically following someone isn't critical. We had a tag on the car."

"So, what does my personal life have to do with your work or assignment?" he asked, now worried that they might blackmail him.

"We were initially concerned you were traveling to Morocco to share sensitive research information. You were a single guy from Boston, on a quick trip, in the middle of winter, and work in science and research. But it has become clear to us you were here for personal reasons."

"So, all's well and good, right?"

"Well, not exactly," Pierre noted. "We are wondering if you might be interested in working with us, for us?"

Brian was shocked and alarmed. "What do you have in mind?"

"There's still a lot of risk that sensitive and lucrative research findings could get passed through Morocco. If your friend Omar takes a job here, you two are in an unparalleled context to sniff out rogue scientists who are looking to make a quick buck."

"I don't get it."

"Omar can't be openly gay in Morocco – particularly at the level of work he's going to do with the government and with the Saudis."

"Go on," Brian nodded, surprised they knew so much.

"He's in love with you."

"I'm not sure about that, but go on."

"If Omar comes to visit you in Boston, you might be able to sniff out scientists who approach him with offers," Pierre noted.

Deborah put her hand on Pierre's forearm and then interjected, "If Omar is working at the center of a secret project here but also travels to Boston from time to time – for business or for pleasure," she winked at Brian, "it would be easier to notice inappropriate attempts to sell information if we had someone like you on the front line, so to speak."

"I couldn't do that," Brian said defiantly. "If – and it is a big if – Omar and I were seeing each other, it would be wrong to take advantage of him in that way. It would be using him for some other purpose."

"We wouldn't want you to do that," Deborah said warmly. "We would just want to make sure that scientists in Boston aren't sharing restricted research information in Morocco. If you and Omar are close, you would be in an ideal position — an inside position — to sniff out illegal attempts to share information."

"It would still be a betrayal of our confidence. I couldn't do it. Besides, if he takes the position here, it's unlikely we will remain connected."

156 ~ MICHAEL HARTWIG

"That's not what we observed," Deborah said pointedly, but with warmth.

"There's no way he could be out here in Morocco."

"Precisely," Deborah nodded. "A long-distance relationship with a lover in Boston is perfect. He has the cover or respectability here, visits you from time to time in Boston, and you will be able to monitor any overtures from US companies toward him. We could even arrange convenient pretexts for his travel."

"You guys have given this some thought," Brian said, feeling quite exposed.

"Things have fallen into place nicely and unexpectedly, we must say," Pierre added, smiling at Deborah.

Brian glanced off into the distance in thought. "I can't do it."

"Of course," Deborah said thoughtfully. "We understand the reluctance. There's no pressure. If you change your mind, you can contact us."

Brian didn't like the look on Pierre's face. The idea of international intrigue over scientific secrets fascinated him, but he didn't like the notion that his relationship with another man might be exploited or scrutinized.

Pierre noted, "You don't have to decide now. We can wait to see how things develop and be in touch. Someone from our office will contact you in Boston."

Brian wasn't relieved by Pierre's assurances and feared future pressure. Deborah stood and looked warmly at Brian, extending her hand. "*C'était un plaisir.*"

Brian wasn't sure he shared her sentiments, but affirmed them, saying, "The pleasure was all mine."

Pierre nodded and took Deborah's hand and walked toward the front of the hotel. Brian took the elevator to his room and called Sherbrooke. "*Allô,*" Hakim responded as he accepted the call.

"*Hakim, c'est Brian.*"

"*Je sais.* I saw your name on the screen. *Et Omar*, how is he?"

"He's fine. He's being recruited for a position here. He's very excited."

"And you?"

"I'm fine," Brian said unconvincingly. "I'll head home tomorrow."

There was a long pause on the other end of the line. Hakim detected Brian's sadness. He asked, "Are you flying Air Canada back from Paris? That's a popular flight."

Hakim impressed Brian with his subtlety and discretion. He realized Hakim was giving him Omar's flight information.

"No," Brian said. "I'm heading to Boston. Connections are better through London."

"Ah, yes. I've heard Air Canada has a nice schedule from the UK as well. Part of the old Commonwealth, you know. I actually think those flights arrive earlier in Montreal than the one from Paris."

"Well, thanks for the tip. I hope to see you again soon."

"*Moi aussi*," Hakim said, the warmth and sincerity evident even over the phone.

Brian got ready for bed and laid on top of the covers staring at the ceiling. He pondered the strange circumstances that had been thrown his way. He had successfully located Omar, only to learn that he was probably moving to Morocco. He had finally pushed himself past the pain and disappointment of Eric's betrayal and his parents' rejection, only to have his new relationship unravel as quickly as it began.

Pierre and Deborah's startling offer unnerved him. As he thought about it, his heart raced. Even taking Omar out of the equation, could he ever be a spy? He wasn't sure he was cut out for the intrigue and danger, even if it held some allure. If by some remote chance he and Omar remained romantically connected, could he ever justify monitoring Omar's professional contacts?

Brian tried to fall asleep but couldn't. Conflicting thoughts and emotions swirled in his head. He tossed and turned, squeezed his pillows tightly, but couldn't erase the image of Omar walking away into the Botanical Gardens. Around three, he fell asleep.

The next morning, he packed, checked out, and took a taxi to the airport. He fully expected to run into Omar, although Omar had an earlier flight through Paris. As he approached the counter, he pondered what Hakim had said about an Air Canada connection through London. He asked the agent, "Is there a possibility of changing my ticket from Boston to Montreal?"

The agent typed into the computer and asked, "So, you want your final destination to be Montreal, not Boston?"

Brian nodded.

"Too bad. There was a flight through Paris that just departed."

"Hm. And the one through London?"

"There's room and, since you are in business class, we can make the change with only a minor fee."

"When does it arrive?"

"It actually arrives earlier than the connection through Paris. There's a shorter layover."

"Let's do it," Brian said without hesitation.

On board the flight to London, Brian dozed off and on. He was physically and emotionally tired, and eased back in his seat, letting the gentle turbulence rock him to sleep. In London, he made his connection with time to spare. He walked up to a bar and ordered a large glass of wine. "It's going to take a lot of liquor to get through the next six hours," he murmured to himself.

The woman next to him must have overheard him and said, "Yes, dear. I totally understand. I get so nervous flying."

"Oh, I'm not afraid of flying. I even like the turbulence. What I don't like is the interminable time in the air, waiting to arrive and reconnect with loved ones."

She stared at him as if he had two heads. She nodded guardedly.

Brian downed his drink and walked toward the departure gate. The crowd was a mix of anglophones and francophones – a beautiful blend of languages that historically had been separated by only a narrow channel. His heart skipped a beat as he looked at the gate monitor and saw the word Montreal instead of Boston. What had possessed him, he asked, as they called for first and business class passengers to board.

He found his seat, unpacked his iPad, hoping he might distract himself with a book. After the flight took off, he ordered another drink and quickly fell asleep.

Five hours later, he woke. He looked out the window at the frozen landscape below. The plane began its descent, with Quebec off to the left, what was once a tiny settlement perched high above the Saint Lawrence River. As the plane landed farther west in Montreal, Brian realized he didn't have a plan. He passed through border and customs patrol, retrieved his luggage, and made his way into the main terminal. He looked at the monitor and noticed the Air Canada flight from Paris arriving in 30 minutes.

15

Chapter Fifteen - Painful Reunion

Brian waited by the exit for international travelers. His heart raced with anticipation. He hadn't been this nervous since his doctoral defense – the sensation that one's life was about to be launched and the apprehension that there could be a misfire or scrub of the mission. He adjusted his scarf and coat, ran fingers through his hair, and popped a few breath mints into his mouth.

A wave of passengers exited the doors with tags from Paris. Suddenly, Omar appeared. His distinctive eyes and endearing face were now familiar, and Brian felt a rush of warmth course through his chest. Brian waved. Omar noticed him. His eyes glistened with surprise, excitement, joy. He set down his bag, ready to approach quickly when the brilliance of his orbs faded, his brows furrowed, and his glowing skin turned ashen.

Brian followed his glance to a couple standing nearby, a man and woman clutching each other, their eyes watering at the sight of their son.

Omar halted abruptly, vacillating between two destinations. Dutifully, he walked towards his mother and gave her a warm embrace and kisses on her cheeks. He gave his father a manly hug and smiled nervously.

He glanced at Brian and walked his parents toward him. Brian had lost all sensation in his legs and felt as if he were about to faint.

"Mom and dad, this is Brian, a colleague from Boston."

Amir shook Brian's hand strongly, jolting Brian back into his body. He took a deep breath.

"Yes. We've heard about him from Hakim. Thanks for checking in on Omar. It brought us much relief."

Omar looked at Brian nervously and said, "Mom and dad, can you excuse us for a moment?"

They nodded. Omar walked away from them and waved Brian forward.

"*Qu'est-ce que tu fais ici?*"

"What am I doing?" Brian repeated his question in disbelief. "What does it look like I'm doing? I'm welcoming you back."

"*C'est pas possible* – it's not possible – not this, not anything," Omar said sternly.

"What do you mean?"

"*Ce que je viens de dire – c'est impossible!*"

"You took the job," Brian concluded. "And you're going to marry."

Omar nodded without emotion.

"But how? How can you do that to yourself?" Brian pleaded.

Omar stared at him stoically and without explanation. He extended his hand and said, "It has been an honor to meet you. I wish you all the best." He then returned to his parents, took them in his arms, and walked away from Brian toward the parking garage.

In shock, Brian began to tremble. He pulled his own bag behind him and sat down on a nearby bench. He leaned forward, holding his head low, near his knees, and took deep breaths. A security guard approached and asked, "*Monsieur, vous allez bien?*"

"*Oui, ça va.*" But, in reality, he was not okay. He felt like his world had been pulled out from under him. He had been riding a wave of euphoria and excitement, ready to embrace Omar and pick up where they left off in Rabat, free in Montreal to express their affection and discuss ways to forge a future together, one way or another. Omar brought the house down, a resounding and unequivocal repudiation of the initial steps they had taken.

"*Cazzo,*" he exclaimed in Italian. He was now angry. He stood up, grabbed his bag, and walked out to the taxi stand. He directed the driver to take him to a hotel in the Vieux Port of Montreal, one he had stayed in before. It was cozy and quiet this time of the year.

Once inside, the front desk clerk, a cute 20-something-year-old, batted his eyes at Brian and said, "Of course we have room for you, Doctor LeBlanc." He gave him a nice suite and complimentary beverage passes for the bar.

Brian went up to his room, unpacked, and felt the pangs of jetlag setting in. He ordered a light dinner from room service, consumed it quickly, and fell into a troubled but deep sleep.

The next day, he logged onto his work email, took care of business, and then began to compose an email to Omar. Nothing sounded right, so he texted him.

"Omar. What the fuck!" He looked at the text and then deleted it.

"Omar. It was good to see you. Sorry things didn't work out." He glanced at it, paused, and deleted it as well.

"Omar. I know you must have reasons for what you are doing. Can we at least talk? I'd like to hear more about your exciting opportunities."

It was a more measured message. He hoped to entice Omar to at least have a conversation, and the final version of his text was less off-putting. He pushed 'send,' and heard the swoosh on his phone.

He didn't expect that Omar would respond immediately and made plans to take a walk. He had always wanted to visit the archaeological museum, and after showering and dressing, walked outside into the bitter cold and walked a short distance to the Pointe-à-Callière museum built on the ruins of some of the first French settlements along the St. Lawrence.

The museum was everything he had hoped it would be – creative, informative, and distracting. In addition to artifacts, the museum included foundations from some of the earliest settlements. Time passed swiftly, and he exited the complex in time for a light lunch. There were many options, and he settled for a small creperie where he enjoyed some ham and bechamel filled crepes, followed by dessert crepes oozing with dark chocolate. A couple of glasses of red wine helped wash it all down. Before returning to the hotel, he checked emails and messages and found nothing from Omar.

He typed in a new message: "Omar. I need to speak with you. I am in Montreal one more night. I will be at the Vieux-Port Steakhouse tonight at 7 PM. I will be waiting."

He noticed the message had been delivered and read. Despite his hope for one, there wasn't a response. After doing some work and taking a nap, he woke around four and took a taxi to Rue Sainte-Catherine to do some shopping. He loved the shopping district of downtown Montreal – the bustle of people walking in and out of shops and the light snow that added a festive feel to the area. He found a new pair of jeans and a European-designed sweater. He returned to the hotel, did some work, took a shower, and then put on his new clothes, carefully brushing his hair, and doing everything he could to look his best for Omar. Brian was certain he would show.

At 6:45, he walked to the restaurant where he had made a

164 - MICHAEL HARTWIG

reservation. It was a classic old-Montreal dining room with stone walls and beamed ceiling. The food was good, and the place was close to his hotel and dimly lit, a perfect venue for a discreet and intense conversation. The servers sat him at an out-of-the-way table. He ordered a bottle of red wine and checked his email nervously.

At 7:00, his heart began to pound, and he felt himself perspire in anticipation of Omar's arrival. He murmured to himself, "You're like a teenager on a date. Get a hold of yourself."

At 7:15, he grew anxious that Omar wouldn't show. He clung to every thread of hope – 'he hadn't responded no' and 'he read the text' and 'he can't just ignore this.'

At 7:30, he was officially depressed, disappointed, and disillusioned. Omar was intelligent. How could he make such a stupid decision? What happened to the lofty ideas of reason and religion? Brian ordered a filet with a salad and opened his ever-trusty dating app. He scrolled through the images of local Quebecois men. Two caught his attention – one a dark, bearded muscle boy who had posted images of his pecs and firm round buttocks – and the other, a cute, thin, adorable man with dreamy eyes and a sensuous mouth. He was about to send a message to the muscular one, when the door of the restaurant pushed open, and Omar appeared.

He opened his jacket and unwrapped his scarf, looking around the dining area. Brian gasped. Omar was disheveled and sullen. He had dark rings under his eyes, and when he spoke with the maître d', he was stern, stoic, and lifeless. The maître d' pointed Brian's direction, and Omar walked toward the table.

Brian closed the app, set down the phone, and embraced Omar guardedly. "I'm glad you came."

Omar nodded, but said nothing. He took a seat.

The server brought a glass, and Brian poured him some wine.

"I was beginning to think you weren't going to come."

"I wasn't," Omar said matter-of-factly.

"And? What changed your mind?"

"I was on the highway heading to Quebec City from my parents' house. When I got to the highway between Montreal and Quebec City, it was as if the car had a mind of its own. I skipped the exit for Quebec City and took the one for Montreal."

Brian nodded, encouraging Omar to elaborate.

"I got here a while ago and drove around. I didn't think I had the courage to come, but here I am."

Omar's face was filled with apprehension and ambivalence. Just below the surface, Brian sensed a smile struggling to break through his reticence. Omar's eyes darted back and forth, avoiding contact. Omar's skin, usually dark and warm, appeared pale and cold.

"I'm glad you're here. We should talk," Brian said softly, invitingly.

"I know," Omar said, staring down at the table.

There was a long pause. Brian was afraid Omar was going to get up and leave and said, "So, you're taking the job in Rabat?"

Omar nodded. "Yes. It's an excellent opportunity." At first, he didn't elaborate. His body lacked passion and excitement. He took a deep breath and continued, "They want me to lead the university's efforts to launch a research center in collaboration with the one in Quebec City. They want to take the lead amongst Arab and Muslim countries in quantum technology. I will be able to teach theoretical physics and lead the research work."

"That's great. I'm sure it is a wonderful opportunity."

Omar smiled guardedly.

"By the way, do you want something to eat?" Brian offered.

Omar shook his head. "My stomach is in knots. I'm not sure I can hold anything down."

"What about a *petit filet*, plain? Eat what you can. It will be good for you."

Omar nodded. Brian waved the server down and ordered a small filet with *frites*.

"*Merci*," Omar said.

"Why is your stomach in knots?"

"Excitement and dread."

"I imagine the excitement has to do with the job and opportunity. What is the dread about?"

"You know."

Brian shook his head no, although he knew what Omar feared.

"I told them I was engaged. That I would bring my wife when I moved there in early summer."

"I can imagine that would cause all sorts of dread."

Omar couldn't contain a nervous smile.

"So, you're going to marry Lara?" he asked, referring to someone Omar mentioned a couple of times.

Omar nodded, looking off into the distance.

"I've been thinking about this, Omar," Brian began hesitantly. "I was impressed back in Rabat when you spoke about *tawhid* and the necessity that science and revelation be consistent. It is not an ideal or aspiration. It is required."

Omar nodded and smiled. He was impressed that Brian remembered their conversation and its particularities.

"What I don't understand is why that doesn't apply to sexuality?"

Omar looked perplexed. He reached for his glass of wine and took a sip. The server came with their steaks. Brian looked up at him and said, "*Bon appétit.*"

Omar nodded, raised his glass, and then took his steak knife and began cutting a piece of the rare meat. Brian followed suit. They took their first bites. "Hm, delicious," Brian said.

Omar replied, "*Vraiment.*"

"So, back to sexuality – why doesn't *tawhid* apply to sexuality?" Brian reiterated his question.

"What do you mean?"

"You're a scientist and believe that the world as created or imagined by God is consistent with what God reveals in the Qur'an, right?"

Omar nodded.

"That's bold and visionary."

Omar smiled.

"So, if God created or imagined a world with sexual diversity, shouldn't the revelation in the Qur'an affirm that, or at least not negate it?"

Omar paused. He furrowed his forehead. "*Peut-être*. But perhaps sexual diversity is a mirage, one that our permissive society has created."

Brian squinted his eyes in disbelief. "You really think that is the case? Haven't you tried to change, to be straight, to ask Allah to help you? And the results?"

Omar blushed.

"Precisely. I know the story all-too-well. Good religious boy discovers he likes dicks and prays to God it isn't true. He still likes dicks and prays that God will change him. God is cruel and doesn't. Good religious boy can't imagine God is cruel, so he believes he hasn't tried hard enough to be normal. He continues to make the efforts, only to fall fatally short. Do I have the story right?"

Omar stared at Brian without emotion.

"All the scientific research shows that there is a percentage of the population that is constitutionally gay – whose sexual fantasies and desires and experiences are homosexual. It is statistically consistent – whether you are in a permissive society or one that is religiously and morally conservative. It is incontrovertible – like the double split experiment. You keep repeating the experiment, thinking you've done it wrong or missed something. The results are the same. It is the same with sexual diversity."

"Maybe you have a point, but I'm not gay."

"Omar. Can you really say that? Have you ever had sex with a woman?"

Omar blushed.

"I didn't think so."

"It's a sin to have sex before marriage."

"That doesn't address the issue. Who do you desire? What will sustain your affections?"

"My work, my children, my family."

"Those sound like obligations to me. Where does love figure into the equation?"

"Love is obligation."

"Ah. Interesting. If I recall, the Qur'an says that Allah created spouses or companions so that we could find comfort and peace and that Allah has engendered love and tenderness between them, between spouses or companions."

Omar raised his eyebrow in surprise. "How do you know that?"

"If I'm going to date a Muslim, I had better educate myself."

Omar smiled, then frowned.

Brian continued. "Allah doesn't talk about obligation. Allah speaks of love, tenderness, companionship. Can you experience that or sustain that with a woman?"

Omar's eyes watered. He shook his head. His lips quivered. Then he said, "But what about my family? I can't lose them."

"Omar, if they love you, they will love you as you are. If they love you based on a façade, is that really love?"

Omar shook his head, a tear streaking down his cheek. Brian wanted to wipe it with his finger, but held back, cognizant of Omar's discomfort.

"You told me you wanted to be a cutting-edge Muslim scientist, one who would restore the grandeur of the ancient Islamic tradition of integrating science and revelation. While I have no doubt you will do this in theoretical physics, what about other areas of science? Why not spark a revolution – an Islamic renaissance – one that shows to the world that reason and revelation can be and must be consistent and, if so, whatever we know through the best of sociology, psychology, and biology can be integrated with the Qur'an."

"But how would that work with homosexuality?" Omar asked with an inquisitive and sincere look.

"Take the passage I mentioned earlier. I believe it is Sura 30, verse 20."

"Now you are scaring me! You're quoting the Qur'an - Sura and verse?"

Brian nodded. "Allah says he created mates, spouses, companions – there are several ways of translating the original Arabic."

Omar nodded.

"Companions create peace and love and tenderness, right?"

"Yes, that's what the passage says."

"So, if through science we know that two men or two women can become companions and create peace, love, and tenderness between them, why can't this be reconciled with Islam as good, holy, acceptable?"

"Well, that's not the only passage. There are passages about Lot and Allah's anger. There are hadith or sayings of Mohammed about punishment of two men caught in the act."

"The story of Lot is in the Jewish scriptures, too. The story doesn't refer to loving gay couples but to men who seek to do sexual violence to other men – to rape them. That's not a disapproval of homosexuality but a condemnation of sexual aggression."

Omar nodded reluctantly.

"And the hadith are ambivalent. Is Mohammed upset with homosexuality or with adultery, presumably because the men having sex are also married to women?"

"You've been doing a lot of reading."

"I was inspired and motivated by someone who is visionary, who wants to spark a new integration of reason and religion. I also happen to love him, and I hope he might love me back."

Omar could feel his heart melt at Brian's words and struggled to maintain the shield he had erected. He longed to lean over and give Brian a deep, warm, affectionate kiss. He was grateful for Brian's insights and concern but feared he would have to journey into perilous terrain. He held back.

"I'm curious. If the university and government in Morocco knew you were gay, would they still offer you the job? Aren't you the most qualified? Aren't they afraid of losing you? The efforts they made to protect you from me — allegedly a spy from MIT — were formidable."

Omar looked off into the distance. "I don't know. I'm not sure I want to find out."

"If you have to compromise your truth for the job, are you willing to do it?"

Omar's eyes darted nervously around the room.

"Omar. How can you advance truth if you are denying your own?"

Omar's eyes watered. "I don't want to lose this opportunity."

"Which one?"

Omar recoiled in his seat, startled by the piercing directness of Brian's line of questioning. He became resentful for Brian's keen precision and observations. He folded his napkin and murmured, "This was a mistake."

"No, Omar. It is not a mistake. You are being presented with a unique opportunity – one that combines your authentic self with your faith tradition. You have the talent to imagine new paradigms. Are you courageous enough to do it?"

Omar shook his head.

"It's not easy. You're embarking on a path few have taken. That is what visionaries do."

Omar looked pensive.

"But you are not alone. I'm here with you in support."

Omar wrestled with his emotions. Intellectually, everything Brian said was true, and it was inspiring. He also realized Brian was a formidable ally in science and in challenging old religious views. But to let his heart go, to let Brian love him, felt like a chasm, a cliff, a precipice. Who would catch him?

"Let me give it some thought," Omar said timidly, hoping to buy time.

"That's all I wanted to hear."

"I'm so afraid."

"That's okay. Again, you're in unchartered terrain."

"I don't know if I can do it."

"You can," Brian said emphatically. "And I would suggest you speak with Hakim."

Omar gave Brian a scrutinizing look.

"Yes. Hakim. I think he can soften up the family, helping them at least consider things they might not have imagined."

"Hm," Omar murmured.

They finished their steaks, ordered coffee, and then stared at each other, wondering what was next.

Omar wanted to be held, to be told it would all be okay. He wanted to feel Brian's strength encircling him, protecting him.

Brian wanted nothing more than to bring Omar back to his room, undress him, and devour him. He ached to run his lips over Omar's skin, to breathe in the unique aroma of his body and to feel the warmth of Omar's dark skin pressed against his.

Omar feared that if he accompanied Brian, there would be no turning back, and he wasn't ready to take that leap. Brian sensed Omar's reticence and decided it was unwise to press him. He wasn't sure he could take the rejection. It was better to leave things ambivalent.

They walked out onto the cobblestone street. A few flurries danced in the lamplight. Both turned to each other and tried to conceal their vacillation, glancing off into the distance.

"Well, Brian. Thanks for the conversation."

Brian stared at Omar in disbelief. His remarks sounded like the conclusion of a business meeting. He could almost predict what Omar would say next. It did not surprise him when Omar continued, "Let's stay in touch."

"Yes, let's do," Brian replied, resigned to an unhappy ending. He reached over and embraced Omar. Omar kissed Brian affectionately on the cheek and pulled away. He turned and walked down the street. He glanced over his shoulder. His beautiful eyes were sullen and watery. Brian turned quickly away to hide his own tears.

16

Chapter Sixteen - Problems in Morocco

Several months later, Omar sat across from Aman in his office at the university. Aman was disappointed, angry, irritated. His breathing was labored, and he kept clearing his throat and loosening his tie. Omar's legs shook, and he rubbed his hands nervously over his thighs.

"I can't believe you were so careless," Aman repeated several times. "I won't be able to clean this up again. The administration's tolerance is limited."

"I'm sorry," Omar said, beads of sweat forming on his forehead.

"Do you realize how dangerous your behavior was? You could have been hurt, blackmailed, or imprisoned. Our initiative could be sabotaged, funding cut off."

Omar turned red with embarrassment and nodded.

Aman stood up and paced, staring at the floor, then out the window, and then back at Omar.

"I thought you were engaged. When are you going to marry?"

"I am. I'm waiting for the right time. I needed to get established first."

"I think the time is now."

Although Aman knew married men occasionally had indiscretions with other men, Omar's behavior was particularly egregious and problematic. He had been carrying on a relationship with one of the male graduate students. They got caught by another student who was religiously conservative and reported it to the police. It was because of the guilty student's parents' status in the government that their arrest was avoided, but the parents demanded swift action against Omar, who they accused of seducing and corrupting their son.

"I will go back to Quebec and make arrangements."

"I suggest you do that immediately. Don't return without a wife."

Omar felt the feeling leave his feet and his stomach tighten in knots. Ibrahim was all he had ever dreamed of in a romantic partner. He was adorable — a lanky, dark, and energetic man. He had bright eyes and a warm, jovial smile. His skin was soft and became intensely hot when they touched. He was well-endowed and highly imaginative when they made love.

They shared a passion for physics – Omar for theory and Ibrahim for its application in new technologies. Ibrahim was creative and could envision things others had never considered. The university and scientific community were ecstatic with the rapid progress of their collaboration.

It had been easy to conceal their relationship. Other research assistants put in their hours, but Omar and Ibrahim remained at the school under the pretext of deadlines to be met. Omar's on-campus apartment was cozy and had a well-equipped kitchen where they would cook and enjoy dinner together. Ibrahim often stayed over, wrapped in Omar's arms.

Both were engaged, and both realized that at some point they would have to marry. They strategized about how to sustain their relationship even while married, even while setting up separate households. Both imagined traveling to conferences together, using their time away to reconnect and kindle their affection.

"What will happen to Ibrahim?" Omar asked.

Aman shook his head. "I don't know. I imagine his parents will conceal this to protect their own status in the government. He will undoubtedly be forced to marry. We will assign him to another project."

"But our collaboration is so fruitful."

"Yes. I know. That is the shame in this all. I can't afford the whole initiative unraveling over your stupidity and indulgence. We'll find you another assistant who is equally talented. But you must first marry. Do I make myself clear?"

"Perfectly," Omar responded.

"How will you handle the student who reported us?"

"Delicately. I'll have to convince him that what he witnessed was an indiscretion, that it doesn't represent who you both are, or perhaps that it was not what it appeared to be."

"But, as you know, we work with him."

"I know. If we move him, that will be a problem. You're going to have to do what you can to dissemble your relationship with Ibrahim. I trust you will be enterprising in making it look like something else."

"I'll do my best."

"I can't emphasize enough how much is at stake. We have invested so much in this project and in recruiting you. Don't disappointment me any further."

"I won't," Omar assured him.

Aman sighed and his shoulders relaxed. Omar took both as a

positive sign that Aman's anger was dissipating. He then asked, "Shaykh Aziz, I have a question."

"Yes," Aman replied impatiently.

"We share an interest in advancing science within Islam, right?"

Aman nodded. "Of course, we do. That's why you're here."

"Why wouldn't the science of sexuality count in that endeavor?"

"I don't know what you mean?" Aman said, clearing his throat.

"Well, there has been a lot of research about sexual orientation, for example."

Aman did not look happy with Omar's direction but remained curious.

"There are scientists who have done studies on sexual orientation, on differences in gay people, genetic and physiological differences. These studies show it is not chosen, it is something one discovers as a given, as part of one's nature."

"Regardless, it is a pathology," Aman interjected quickly.

"That's possible. That something has a genetic basis doesn't mean it is automatically good. Cancer is genetically different from healthy cells, but we regard it as a pathology."

"Exactly," Aman said, as if proving a point.

"But there are also sociologists and psychologists who study gay people, gay families, and gay parenting. Over the years, in the light of these studies, they have removed homosexuality from the list of pathologies," Omar said.

Aman's smile turned to a frown. He bristled at the use of the term homosexuality and shifted in his seat at Omar's line of discourse.

Omar continued. "If two gay people were unable to love each other authentically, if they were inevitably unhappy and troubled, we might say their condition was pathological. But when we see two men or two women form a long-term loving relationship – with evidence of fidelity, generosity, compassion, and love, how can this be considered an illness, something wrong?"

"It's against the natural order. Allah created man and woman."

"In the Qur'an, Allah says he created companions or spouses for love and tenderness," Omar said, recalling Brian's observations months before.

"That means man and woman," Aman noted.

"But if Allah intended love and tenderness and if two men or two women who become companions achieve that, why wouldn't that reflect God's creation?"

"It's unnatural. It is contrary to nature."

"But science has shown same-sex attraction is part of natural sexual diversity. It isn't a practice that arises in permissive or sinful societies. Sexual orientation is not a choice. It exists as a percentage of the population everywhere. It is part of creation, part of the world as we know it."

"But Allah condemns it."

"Allah doesn't condemn it. The story of Lot condemns sexual violence. Doesn't the concept of *tawhid* apply here – that what Allah reveals and what Allah creates must be consistent?"

"Yes. That's why science is compatible with Islam."

"So, why doesn't science regarding sexuality apply as well?"

"The evidence you cite is inconclusive. Homosexuality is not natural or good; it is a pathology. Two men together is merely indulgent – it's selfish and irresponsible. It undermines other institutions that sustain a good society."

Omar shook his head. He realized his mentor and patron would not budge. He sat sternly, staring at Omar, and added, "I expect you to return to Quebec, get married, and bring your wife back to Rabat."

Omar nodded, but he couldn't imagine marrying Lara.

Aman stood and extended his hand. Omar rose and shook Aman's hand. He turned and walked out of the office into the hallway.

Aman walked back around his desk. Adrenaline was racing

through his body, and he was shaking. He was angry at Omar. But more to the point, Omar had stirred deep and painful memories. He pulled open the upper right-hand drawer of his desk and pulled out a worn photograph of a young student – someone who had an uncanny resemblance to Omar, Omar's grandfather. Aman rubbed his fingers over the portrait as he had done countless times before. He closed his eyes and imagined the scent of his lover, the softness of his caramel skin, the hardness of his sex aroused, and the stimulating conversations they used to have after making love.

The traumatic and abrupt end of their relationship, thirty-something years earlier, continued to haunt him. The discovery of Kahlid Aziz in the arms of a high-level government official prompted a swift bribe paid to him to leave Morocco and establish a business in Quebec. There had been no opportunity for Aman and Kahlid to say goodbye. Aman was content with a few letters written over the years and, more recently, with the opportunity to follow his children and grandchildren on the internet and through social media. But he missed his friend, someone who made his pulse race and who brought peace and calm to his troubled heart.

His eyes watered. A tear streaked down his cheek and landed on the photograph. Over the years, he wondered if he had made the right decision to remain in Morocco and not immigrate to Quebec with Khalid. He sacrificed love for his career and for the respect and privilege he enjoyed as a professor and shaykh. After Kahlid departed, Aman had never touched another man – or woman. He sublimated all of his sexual energy into his teaching and his leadership in the local Muslim community. People appreciated how available he was, and how his resources were spent mentoring new scientists rather than supporting a family.

Omar's remarks stirred his own youthful idealism, the search for change in Islam, an ability to celebrate sexual differences, to embrace love. Indeed, he had even written draft articles on science and

Islam and sexuality, and all of Omar's remarks were on target. But change was not possible, and his whole life's sacrifices and purpose were on the line. No, Omar would have to do as he had done. He would have to do his duty and make changes where he could, not where they were culturally impossible.

Omar returned to his apartment. He logged onto his computer to book a flight home. He scrolled to his photos and clicked on Lara's. She was beautiful. She had dark silky hair, a beautifully shaped face, delicate shoulders, and full, round breasts. They had never made love, but he imagined they could. He would have to imagine Ibrahim's soft buttocks as he slid himself into Lara. He would close his eyes and imagine Ibrahim's full sensual lips and the wetness they shared as they kissed deeply.

She shared his love of family, traditions, and children. They would have a large family. She would keep busy at home and he at the university. They would help the family reconnect with their Moroccan roots, their parents, aunts, uncles, and cousins coming for visits and excursions to the beach. His university position compensated well, and they would have a good life.

Omar selected a flight for the next day and emailed his parents. They would be ecstatic. He would contact Lara on return, and they would discuss arrangements. Yes, it all made sense. It wasn't what he imagined or wanted, but it could work, it had to work.

17

Chapter Seventeen - Family Meeting

A week later, Omar pulled up to Hakim's house. It was the largest of the extended family and the place where holidays and special occasions took place. It was fall, and the leaves were brilliant. Bright orange, yellow, and red foliage clung to the thick branches of maple trees lining the street. The yards were covered in a quilt of fallen leaves, and a brisk wind blew them along the pavement.

His parents' car was in the driveway behind Hakim's, and his uncles' cars were parked on the street. Omar's hands were cold, and he couldn't feel the tips of his toes. He dreaded what was about to transpire, but realized it needed to happen, whatever the outcome.

He knocked and then opened the front door. Everyone looked up as he entered, smiling excitedly. The men all wore jackets, and the women had chosen their finest garments and scarves. The room smelled of perfume.

Hakim and his wife Aisha were closest to the door, rose, and embraced Omar. His own father, Amir, cleared his throat. He took his wife's hand, rose, and held his son's arm affectionately. Omar kissed his mother, Nebila.

"Where's Lara?" his mother asked, looking behind Omar and over his shoulder. She looked worried.

Omar glanced at Hakim, who nodded.

Omar felt his throat constrict. He took a deep breath and said, "She's not coming."

His mother stared at her son, hoping for an explanation.

Omar glanced at the rest of the room. Malik and Nura and Nassen and Zaina were chatting. As the room got quiet, they looked up at Omar.

"Omar, welcome back! How is Morocco?" Nassen asked enthusiastically, not picking up on the growing concern over Lara's absence.

"It's nice," Omar said without emotion or elaboration.

"Are they treating you well?" Malik inquired.

Omar nodded.

Aisha nodded to Zaina, who rose. They went into the kitchen to make coffee.

Malik said, "How was the trip from Quebec?"

"Fine," Omar replied. He cleared his throat and added, "There wasn't much traffic."

Amir and Nebila whispered in each other's ears, glancing periodically at their son with inquisitive looks.

"Omar, have a seat," Hakim began, pointing to a chair that had been placed to the side all by itself.

Omar took off his jacket, draped it on the back of the chair, and took a seat. It was supposed to be a joyous occasion, the announcement of his marriage. But, as he looked at his aunts and uncles, he felt like he was about to be put on trial, and while currently smiling, he feared their verdict and sentence would be unpleasant once they learned the truth. Aisha and Zaina returned from the kitchen and began pouring coffee and setting out cakes. To break the silence, Omar began asking questions.

"Uncle Malik and Aunt Nura, how is Marwa? Didn't she get a new job in Montreal?"

Nura replied, "She's getting settled. She and her husband Jabir just announced they are going to have a baby in December."

"Congratulations," Omar said warmly. Nura smiled proudly. Malik kept a stern face.

"And Zaina? Are you still working at the mosque?"

She nodded and smiled and glanced nervously at her husband, Nassen. Their sons, Tariq and Hassan, had spotted Brian and Omar in Boston last winter, sparking rumors that still had not been put to rest. They were looking forward to Omar's marriage. They didn't want to believe the earlier allegations.

Everyone began sipping their coffee and looked to Omar and Hakim to begin. Several had been whispering to each other. Hakim took a sip of his coffee and cleared his throat.

"Omar, may I?"

Omar didn't nod or say anything. He was frozen in fear. Hakim sensed it and said, "Omar, we're here to hear more about your time in Morocco and decisions you have in mind. My brothers- and sisters-in-law are here to support you. Tell them what you told me."

Omar knew they were not there to support him. They were guardians of the family and sentinels of tradition. Omar felt his leg shake. He placed his hand on his knee and took a sip of coffee.

He then began, "As I shared with Hakim and my parents, the job in Morocco has been going well. The government has teamed up with scientists in Quebec City to advance new quantum technology. They had been recruiting me for the last year. They were eager to engage someone with Canadian and Moroccan citizenship who speaks French and Arabic, and who has expertise in physics."

"That's wonderful, son," Amir noted. "We're proud of you."

Omar smiled and glanced at his mother, who was smiling.

Malik then added, "And we hear there will be a wedding soon?"

Everyone looked at Omar with eager faces.

"Unfortunately, there will not be a wedding," Omar began, rubbing his hands together.

Amir looked at his wife and then back at their son, furrowing his brows.

"Sorry, mom and dad."

They shook their head as if to say, 'not a problem but explain to us why.'

Omar felt his chest constrict. He wanted to stand and leave, but he knew he had to face the clan.

"Lara and I have called off our engagement," he continued.

Aisha and Zaina nervously looked to see if anyone needed refills for coffee.

"It was a mutual decision. We both realized it wasn't the right fit."

People leaned forward in anticipation of an explanation.

To soften the more significant reasons that he was going to share eventually, Omar added motives that were partially true and easier to digest. "Lara wasn't excited about moving to Morocco. She is close with her family here, and her parents are aging."

Nebila nodded. She had never been that excited about Lara in the first place. Her parents were from another ethnic clan and were not devout Muslims.

Everyone nodded, waiting for Omar to continue.

He cleared his throat. "I am not sure I was a good match for Lara. Over the past several years, I have been struggling with my identity, with my sexual orientation." Omar paused and glanced at Hakim, who gave him a look of encouragement.

"I think I am gay," he said. He let out a long sigh. He had imagined this day and those words for years. It felt like a vice had been taken off his chest as he pronounced the words, named his truth, claimed his voice.

His mother's eyes watered, and his father blushed. Hakim looked each of his brothers in the eye, taking a pulse of things. Nassen was the most unsettled, and Hakim knew why.

Malik interjected, "Sometimes it's a phase." He was trying to be helpful, and Omar appreciated it.

"Uncle Malik, what you say is true in some cases. I thought the same thing. I have asked Allah to change me, but there is no change. This is who I am."

Nassen continued to squirm in his chair. Omar caught his stern look and wondered if he had made a mistake in being so forthcoming.

Hakim cleared his throat again, and as the oldest of the clan, said, "We love you. You are a wonderful young man. You have been a faithful son, and you have worked hard. We can't believe you are the lead scientist for a project in Morocco. We will support you as you continue to make sense of your life."

Omar's eyes watered.

Nassen murmured something to his wife, Zaina. Omar thought he heard the word, *dhanb*, sin, in Arabic. Zaina blushed and looked down to avert any eye contact with her close family.

"Nassen, do you have something to say?" Hakim inquired.

At first Nassen shook his head. Amir, Omar's father, was about to say something when Nassen interjected. "Yes. I do have something to say. We have all been raised Muslim, praise be to Allah. We have studied the Qur'an — the very words of Allah. How can we encourage something Allah has forbidden? It will bring shame and ruin to our family and to our business."

Malik and Amir looked at Nassen, then they glanced at Hakim, looking for direction.

Nassen continued, "We are proud of the opportunity you have

in Morocco, Omar. Don't mess it up. Marry Lara. You will have a happy life and a happy home, insha'Allah."

Everyone repeated, "Insha'Allah."

"Yes, God willing," Hakim said. "But what if God wants something else? What if, as Omar has shared with me, he has pleaded with God to change him, and God hasn't? Who are we to question God's wisdom and God's mercy?"

"What you say, brother, is blasphemous. How can Allah will something Allah has forbidden?"

"How do we know Allah has forbidden Omar's love?" Hakim added.

"It says so in the Qur'an," Nassen said pointedly.

"Where?" Hakim asked in reply.

"The story of Lot, for one."

"I did some reading, brother. The sin of the people in Sodom was sexual violence, rape, not loving relationships between men."

"What about the passage referring to zina?" Nassen continued to press.

Hakim hesitated and looked at Omar. "What is illicit about two men's relations? Is it that they are married and are having sex outside of marriage, or is it that they are two unmarried men who have sex with each other? And is the latter considered a problem since it is sex before marriage? If so, we put gay people in an impossible predicament. They can't marry, so any intimacy they share is zina. If they do marry women and have sex on the side, it is zina. What if two men could marry and genuinely love each other? Would that be zina?"

Nassen stood, put on his coat, looked at his wife and said, "We are leaving. This is too much." He spit on the ground.

Hakim stood and extended his hand toward Nassen and said, "Nassen, wait. I have something to say to you and to our brothers."

Nassen looked anxious, and Omar was now certifiably unnerved.

186 - MICHAEL HARTWIG

Hakim looked over at Omar and then stared at each of his brothers. "It is time for this family to face its past so that it can embrace the future."

They all looked at Hakim as if he had two heads.

"Nassen, I don't know if you remember it or not. When you were about ten, you accidentally witnessed something."

Nassen shook his head. "No, Hakim. Don't."

"You offer me no choice."

"I take back what I said," Nassen pleaded. "Don't."

"Then you do remember. Can you share what you saw, or must I?"

Nassen began to sob.

Malik and Amir looked anxiously at Hakim and at Nassen.

"Our father, rest his soul, was a great man. He was smart, loved his family, and loved Allah. But he and a senior member of the government had a deep affection for each other. One day, Nassen came into our father's office and found him and the government official having sex."

Gasps were heard throughout the room. Hakim had already shared the story with Omar, and Omar felt bad that his uncles' memory of their father was being shattered on his behalf.

Nassen continued to sob. Hakim walked toward him and placed his hand on his shoulder. "It's okay. You've carried the burden of this too long. Let it out."

"I'm sorry," Nassen murmured.

"It's not your fault," Hakim said compassionately. "As a ten-year-old, you took on the guilt of your father. You repressed the memory to save your father, to preserve the image you had of him. That memory has been gnawing at you for decades. It is time to let it go. You didn't cause what you saw, and your father, our father, is still the loving, thoughtful, and brave man he always was."

"But it was horrible," Nassen struggled to say.

"Sex is difficult for any child to witness, whether it is between two men or two women or a man and a woman. Add to that the shame we project onto gay people, and it is no wonder it was traumatic for you."

Malik then asked, "So, what happened? Is that why we ended up coming here?"

Hakim nodded. "Just before his death, dad confided in me. He thought someone should know what really happened."

They all leaned forward.

"The government official, not to be named, was already afraid of rumors about him. He was afraid that Nassen would say something. He provided funds and papers for us to leave Morocco and set up a business here."

"So, there wasn't a problem with another clan?"

Hakim shook his head. "No. It was the fear of exposing someone very high in the government."

Amir then asked, "So, what does this have to do with Omar?"

"History seems to be repeating itself," Hakim began. He looked at Omar, who nodded for him to continue. "Despite his efforts, Omar has been unable to deny his affections. He and a graduate student are in love. They were found out, and Ibrahim's parents have asked the university to intervene."

"Does this mean your job is ending?" Amir asked.

Omar was hesitant to respond, but he answered his father, "Not if I marry Lara and bring her back to Rabat."

Amir was a traditional man, and he wanted to encourage his son to marry, start a family, and be the famous scientist he was destined to be. He realized it might be hard, but he had no doubts his son could pull it off, do his duty, just as Amir's own father had done. Amir leaned forward and was about to speak when his wife, Nebila, interjected. "Son, Allah created spouses for love and tenderness. Your father and I have had a beautiful and loving marriage. We fell in love many years ago, and I still feel the same affection for him now as I did then. I would hate for you to begin a marriage without affection, without tenderness, without passion and love."

Amir and his brothers looked at Nebila incredulously. It was rare that a woman would speak so directly and authoritatively when men were present. She tilted her head and nodded, daring them to challenge her right to speak.

Hakim added, "Brothers, I called you here to see if we can end this terrible cycle."

Malik said, "Our father was happy. He was loving. What is so terrible? Omar has a great job and a beautiful fiancé."

Hakim shook his head. "We are encouraging or forcing Omar to do something contrary to his own nature. He would be entering a relationship with Lara that should be full of affection, tenderness, devotion, and love, but instead, there will be indifference, antipathy, and remorse. Lara will always wonder why her husband is cold and unenthusiastic. Their children who learn that love is more about obligation than affection, about duty rather than passion, and practicalities instead of friendship, play, and joy. That is a shame and tragic."

Omar's father looked compassionately at his son and said, "Omar, what do you want to do?"

"I want to be a great scientist and advance the reputation of Islam."

Omar's father and uncles all nodded and smiled.

"But," he continued, and as he began to formulate words, his uncles' smiles gave way to furrowed brows. "I don't want to be a hypocrite, nor do I want to ruin someone else's life."

"But you will ruin your own," Nassen repeated what he had said earlier.

"I have another offer in Boston. I can pursue my work in science."

"But what about the idea of advancing Islam with your work?" Malik asked.

"That is my dilemma. I must admit the opportunity in Morocco is incredible, but I can't be myself there. And I can't pretend that Islam embraces science and reason in one area when it is blatantly oppressive in another."

Nassen bristled. Hakim leaned forward, ready to come to Omar's aid.

"I'm not asking for your blessing," Omar added. "I wanted to let you know why I have returned to North America, and why I am breaking off my engagement with Lara."

Nassen, Malik, and Amir all shook their head. Hakim nodded encouragingly at Omar and asked, "What are your plans?"

"I've made several calls to Rabat to see if something could be worked out, and there doesn't seem to be the will to embrace change. I return with a wife, or I lose the job."

Omar's mother shook her head, and Amir held her hand, patting his other hand affirmatively on top of the back of her hand. He was coming around.

"I have another offer in Massachusetts, in Cambridge. I initially turned the offer down. That was the time Tariq and Hassan saw me in Boston. I will meet with officials next week."

"That's great news," Hakim noted.

"Yes. It's close enough to come home often, but far enough away so that there are no problems for the family and your business."

Hakim, Malik, Amir, and Nassen looked at each other, aware that if Omar remained in Quebec and began living with a man, they would face repercussions. Omar could see them begin to breathe peacefully again. They appreciated Omar's sensitivity.

Nebila had questions, lots of them. She wondered if the student Omar was involved with in Morocco might immigrate to Boston. She also wondered if what Tariq and Hassan had seen in Boston meant there might be someone else on the scene, the man who they met at the airport months before. She eyed Hakim, who seemed to have a lot of background information. She scrutinized him to see if he might be forthcoming. She didn't dare ask her son directly, certainly not in this context.

Amir stood and said, "Brothers. Does anyone have any other questions? Nebila and I would like to take Omar home. We're looking forward to visiting with him after his extended time away."

Amir's brothers shook their head. All stood and walked to Omar, shaking his hand and giving him guarded embraces. Omar winked at Hakim and thanked him for his guidance.

Omar put his arms around his father and mother, walking toward the door. He grabbed his mother's coat and helped her put it on. He waved to his aunts and uncles and walked outside. They got in their respective cars and drove home.

Omar's family lived in an 80s-era ranch house in a suburb of Sherbrooke. His parents had been frugal, saving money for their children's education. Only recently had they begun to renovate and update their home. Nebila had prepared some food in advance and went into the kitchen to warm it up. Omar sat with his father in the parlor. Amir wrung his hands nervously.

"Dad, I'm sorry to disappoint you," Omar said.

"I'm sorry you're having to struggle with this," Amir said, looking at his son tenderly. "I can't imagine how difficult it must be."

Omar's eyes watered. His tears turned to sobs, and he began to shake uncontrollably.

Amir stood and put his arms around his son and held him tightly.

Omar felt layers of shame and remorse lift from him. Everything he had feared — disappointing his family, being found out, and having to forego his dreams had come crashing down on him. But the firm embrace of his father settled deep within his bones. He began to feel safe and at peace.

His mother returned from the kitchen, setting platters of traditional Moroccan food on the dining table. It was supposed to have been a celebratory dinner with Omar and Lara. She looked over at her husband and to Omar and waved them to the table. "It's ready."

They sat down, and Amir said a blessing in Arabic. Omar wanted a glass of wine to calm his nerves but settled for the warm tea Nebila poured. He took a long sip and felt the warm liquid warm his chest.

"Mom, thanks for what you said at Uncle Hakim's. It meant a lot."

Nebila's countenance had faded. The reality of what her son faced troubled her. She wasn't angry with him but apprehensive, and full of questions.

"What will you do?" she asked.

"I'm going to see if I can get the job in Cambridge. It's a great opportunity."

"And Brian?" she pressed, having met him at the airport earlier in the year.

The mention of Brian startled Omar. He hadn't expected his mother to be so forthright.

"*C'est fini.* It's over."

Amir glanced at his wife, who looked down at her plate and began to push food around. "Hakim mentioned him. He said he was a doctor and a nice man."

Omar nodded.

Amir took a bite of his food and looked up at his son. "We're proud of you. None of us expected that one of our children would become a professor, much less someone being recruited around the world."

Nebila smiled. She cleared her throat. "I hear the gays can get married and have children."

Amir looked at her and shook his head. He wasn't against the idea, but he didn't want to pressure his son further.

"It's true. Even here in Sherbrooke there are gay families," she noted.

Omar continued to eat and drifted off in his thoughts. He thought of Ibrahim and the plans they had concocted to start families but maintain their relationship clandestinely. The idea of marrying with his parents' blessing and starting a family with another man hadn't crossed his mind. He looked at his mother and realized that not only was she capable of accepting the notion, she was actively putting gears in motion to make it happen. She moved quickly.

Omar blushed. They continued to visit. His mother was fearless, asking many questions. Amir listened as his son tried his best to respond to his mother's queries about gay life. They finished dinner. Omar did the dishes, and Amir and his wife settled in the parlor to watch the news. Everyone had tired of the intense discussion.

Omar retired to his room. He was emotionally exhausted, but relieved things went as well as they could. He appreciated his parents' support and realized how fortunate he was. He thought of Ibrahim and the torture he was undoubtedly going through as his conservative parents reprimanded him for his behavior.

Omar scrolled to a photo on his phone. It was one he had taken of Brian on the slopes at Mont-Sainte-Anne. He had taken off his helmet. His dark hair rustled in the light wind and glistened in the bright sun reflecting off the snow. He had unfastened the top of his jacket and was holding one of his ski poles, shifting his weight onto one hip and posing casually as Omar took his picture. He smiled warmly, affably.

Omar ran his fingers over Brian's image, longing to talk with him. It had been months since they had communicated, a tough conversation in Old Montreal. They promised to stay in touch but hadn't. Omar had followed Brian's posts on social media – a cute date on the slopes at Stowe shortly after their visit in Montreal, images of Brian at Broadway with another man, and a lot of photos in the summer of Brian on the beach in Provincetown lying next to countless handsome men in various stages of undress on the warm sand at the edge of the ocean.

Omar set his phone down and leaned his head back on a pillow. He stared at the ceiling and wondered if he was the victim of a cruel joke – if the fates were playing with him. He was back home with his parents. He had no job, no fiancé, and no boyfriend. All the excitement and novelty of a new life in Morocco six months ago had turned to dust. His only hope was that the people in Cambridge might still be interested in bringing him onto their team.

18

Chapter Eighteen - Nassen

Amir entered the garage the next morning. There were many jobs lined up as people prepared for winter. They had requests to mount snow tires, to change oil, to repair engines, to replace new batteries, and a backlog of repairs on crumpled car bodies.

He and his brothers had developed an efficient division of labor. Hakim managed the finances. Malik interfaced with local authorities and insurance. Nassen and Amir took responsibility for the actual work. Nassen and his sons did more of the internal repairs. Amir had a crew of family and outside employees who did body repair.

It was a chilly morning. Amir entered, went to the kitchen area, and poured a warm cup of coffee. Hakim nodded to him from behind his glass office window, and Malik patted him on the shoulder as he passed.

Nassen was busy shouting orders to his sons. He was agitated and short-tempered. He looked up at Amir and gave an almost imperceptible nod. Amir could feel the coldness and reserve in his eyes.

Tariq and Hassan were busy leaning over the motor of a Volvo, passing tools back and forth. Amir passed and said, "*Bonjour. Ça va?*"

"*Ça va,*" they murmured without elaboration or feeling.

Amir went to the lot and examined a car that had been towed the previous day. He shook his head, realizing the repair would be extensive. He rubbed his hand over the crumpled surface. His stomach knotted as he imagined the shock of the driver when she hit the deer – the abrupt force that interrupted her journey, and the loss of life she witnessed as the deer lay trembling on the side of the road.

Amir returned to the inside of the shop. He shared information with Hakim about the scope of work needed. Hakim took notes, then looked up. "Are you okay? After yesterday?"

"It was a bit of a surprise, although I guess I always suspected Omar was a little different. It wasn't the dream Nebila and I had for him, but we know he is making his way, and you have been a great help to him."

"If you need anything, let me know. We're family, and we will deal with this together."

Amir nodded, touched by his oldest brother's support.

Nassen passed Hakim's office. Ordinarily he would have stopped, chatted, shared news. He hurried past. Amir looked at Hakim, who returned a concerned look.

Amir returned to the garage floor and chatted with Tariq and Hassan, asking them when they might be able to do some internal repairs on the new tow. They were not as friendly and talkative as usual, but they were respectful, as they had been taught to be toward their elders.

Nassen walked onto the floor. He mumbled something under his breath. Tariq and Hassan sensed their father's irritation. They buried their noses in their work.

Amir walked toward Nassen and said, "*Comment ça va?*"

He didn't answer.

"*Nassen, tout va bien?*"

Nassen walked toward the tool area and tried to look busy, nodding to Amir distractedly.

"*Nassen, qu'est-ce qui se passe?*"

Nassen turned to Amir. His face was red and stern. "I don't want to talk about it."

"I'm sorry for what you have had to carry all of these years. I never knew."

Nassen turned back to the tools. He shook his head.

Amir walked away, convinced he was only making Nassen feel worse. Nassen turned and grabbed Amir by the shoulder. "It is a sin. You can't make it anything else. It is disgusting, and I will have nothing to do with you or Omar."

Amir was shocked and glared at Nassen.

Nassen stared back, defiantly. "It is an embarrassment to our family, to our business. All of these years, we have worked to establish a reputation for our work and a reputation with our local Muslim community. In one swoop, you are ruining it."

Amir felt adrenaline course through his body and blood rush to his face. The word embarrassment touched a nerve. As Muslims from North Africa, Amir and his brothers had fought the prejudice of the local dominant culture made up of white French and English families who opposed the arrival of Latin American, Caribbean, and African immigrants. Over the years, they worked hard to make friends with the local community and become part of the fabric of Sherbrooke.

"Are you still embarrassed to be a Muslim, to be Moroccan?"

"Of course not."

"Was it easy becoming part of the community?"

"No," Nassen said forcefully. "It took years of work and patience, and I don't want to throw it away."

"So, if you who know the pain and alienation of prejudice can't be compassionate to someone like Omar, who can?"

"It's different."

"How?"

"It's a sin."

"Do you think Omar had a choice? I know my son. He has done everything he could to change his orientation. He has done everything he could to pretend he was straight, to be accepted, to be treated like others. He has done the same that we did at first, downplay our heritage, language, and ethnicity. We couldn't hide, he could. But, in the end, the denial of oneself causes the same pain, the same trauma, the same shame. I've seen how it ate away at our own confidence and happiness. We of all people should be compassionate and understanding and help eradicate irrational prejudices."

"It's one thing to fight against discrimination of race, ethnicity, and religion. But this is too much."

"It's the same thing."

"It's not, and you are a fool to think it is. You've been brainwashed by the liberal secular culture we live in." Nassen spit on the floor.

"And you've been haunted by what you saw and the shame our father and others have projected onto gay people. It's time for that to stop, to end the cycle of shame, hate, and self-abuse. I won't take part in it anymore."

Nassen stared at Amir. Lines in the sand had been drawn, and they both wondered how this would affect their work together.

Hakim had glanced up earlier and witnessed the exchange. He didn't have to hear the words. He knew what had transpired. He walked out onto the floor of the garage. Tariq and Hassan were mouth agape at the exchange between their father and their uncle. They watched Hakim approach Amir and Nassen.

"Brothers. Let's go back into my office."

Nassen shook his head. "I have nothing to discuss."

"We have to work through this," Hakim stated, staring at Nassen and Amir. "We can't let something like this get between us."

"Precisely," Nassen said, his head cocked self-righteously. "We know what is right and what is wrong. Omar needs to be responsible," Nassen concluded.

Hakim peered at Nassen. His eyes had been filled with admonition, but they changed, softened, and became compassionate. He furrowed his forehead and stood quietly in front of him. Then, slowly and purposefully, he walked toward Nassen. He reached his hand toward Nassen's face. Nassen turned his head slightly, a reactive flinch. He felt Hakim's hand touch his upper right brow. Hakim's hands were rough, but they were warm and gentle as he traced his thumb over a long scar hidden just under Nassen's wavy, dark hair.

Nassen's eyes watered, and he trembled, his legs becoming weak. He glanced nervously at his sons, who were astonished as their uncle caressed the side of their father's head. No one had seen the Aziz brothers express affection so tenderly or, for that matter, had they seen two men exchange such a demonstrative gesture. Amir stood quietly in amazement, grasping the significance and reason for Hakim's act.

Nassen collapsed in the arms of Hakim and began to sob. Hakim patted the back of his head, his own eyes filling with tears as he looked up over Nassen's head into Amir's eyes, now watering as well. Hakim could feel the resentment, anger, and shame lift from his brother's shoulders.

Amir walked toward Tariq and Hassan and nodded for them to follow him outside. They stood in the parking lot. It was cold, and they all began to shiver as a few flurries floated in the frosty air.

"Your father is a brave man," Amir began.

"What just happened?" Tariq asked, clearly moved by what they saw.

"Your father is very proud and probably never wanted to alarm you. When we were younger, he was attacked by a gang of local boys. He was on his way home from school, and they had been taunting him about being a camel jockey and dirty Arab. He was a fighter and stood his ground. They were, however, bigger and more numerous, and they wrestled him to the ground. They kicked him forcefully, and one took a knife and cut him along the side of his head."

"That's horrible," Hassan remarked, shaking as adrenaline coursed through his cold body.

"Yes. He staggered home. Our father and mother nursed his physical wounds as best they could. After a few days of recuperation, he returned to school. There was a lot of discussion between my parents about how best to handle the situation – whether to report the boys to school officials, report the incident to the police, or let it go. Nassen didn't want them to report the incident. He claimed he was okay and that he would not let it happen again. He began to carry a knife to school."

"So, nothing was ever done?" Tariq inquired.

"Unfortunately, no. Nassen toughened up. He became angrier, harder, more brazen, and bolder in his demeanor. Somehow, he convinced his assailants that they had much to risk if they tried it again. Unfortunately, the incident left scars – not just physical ones, but emotional ones. Nassen never talked about it again."

"Why would Uncle Hakim touch him like that?" Tariq pressed.

"Your father is carrying around a lot of pain, a lot of shame, what we call post-traumatic stress. It gets projected onto others – in this case, to Omar. I think he wanted him to let it go."

"I don't get it," Hassan noted. "He's upset that Omar is doing something against Islam, something that reflects badly on us. Isn't that reasonable?"

Amir looked off into the distance to give himself time to formulate his thoughts. He turned back to Hassan and Tariq and said, "I think Omar is a trigger. We have been brought up to think that Omar's sexuality is wrong, it's shameful, and it will reflect badly on us as a family and as a business, particularly in our Muslim community. Since your dad has never dealt with his own emotional pain and shame, when he sees it, particularly when it might impact him, it triggers painful memories, memories he has tried to bury for years."

"But isn't that why Omar's behavior is so problematic?"

"How is Omar different from all of us?" Amir began. "We are a different ethnicity and a different religion. Although some local francophones and anglophones embrace us and embrace diversity, many don't. They see us as a threat to their culture or as people who are backward, dirty, a blight on their community. It's easy for us to internalize those feelings and feel inferior. It's easy for us to retreat into our safe community. For Omar, it's the same thing. He can't change or alter his nature. It's different from the dominant heterosexual culture. For centuries, people shamed and judged gay people and feared they would be a stain on their community."

Tariq nodded, but Hassan furrowed his brows. "But sexuality behavior differs from ethnicity."

"Is it? We obviously can't hide who we are. Omar can pass as straight, but it costs him on the inside. Why should we cause that kind of emotional pain?"

"It's just not right," Hassen reiterated. "He needs to suck it up and do the responsible thing."

"I think that's what your father thinks, given how he reacted to the assault he suffered," Amir noted. "I'm not excited about Omar being gay, but all I want for my son is a good life, a good job, and love. Your father didn't challenge his assailants' prejudices. He internalized them. He took them on himself. We're asking Omar to do the same thing – not to challenge biases but to reinforce them by letting them remain in place as if they were reasonable."

"Ethnic discrimination is unreasonable, but standing up for moral values makes sense."

"What are the moral values we stand up for? What are the characteristics of Allah that we seek to embody – fairness, respect, compassion, mercy? If you were gay, how would you want people to treat you?"

"I'm not," Hassan said pointedly.

"But, if one day you woke up and discovered you were – through no choice of your own – how would you want people to treat you? Wouldn't you want people to be understanding?"

"I would change."

"That's the problem. We used to think homosexuality was a behavioral issue. We now know that people are born a certain way. They have no choice over their orientation and forcing them to marry and be straight causes countless problems for them and for their spouses. It's not fair, and it serves no purpose."

Amir could see Hassan's shoulders relax, and Tariq continued to nod affirmatively. Tariq added, "Uncle Amir, we will do what we can to support Omar, won't we?" he asked as he glanced at his brother.

Hassan nodded reluctantly.

"Your father will need your support and understanding," Amir noted. "At the moment, he feels a certain vindication that he's being heroic, that he's resisting the marginalization we struggle with. At some level, Omar's coming out makes him feel superior – he's manned up in a way he thinks Omar should."

"So, how do we help him?"

Amir shook his head. He wasn't a psychologist, and it was difficult to figure out how best to help his brother process things. He began tentatively, "Maybe it's a matter of helping your dad realize it wasn't his fault he was assaulted."

"But it wasn't," Tariq noted emphatically.

"You're right. It wasn't. But since he never reported it, there's a sense in which he has taken on responsibility for it himself."

"That's bizarre," Hassan said.

"We all do things that make little sense. Maybe to avoid additional conflict, it was easier for him to think that he just needed to man up more, to be stronger. To admit that someone took advantage of you is difficult."

"I can see that," Tariq said.

"Omar's decision to come out looks weak to your father. It looks like he's giving in. Your father probably thinks he should be brave, marry Lara, take on the responsibilities that he did. What he doesn't see is his how brave it is to come out, to fight prevailing views and biases. Maybe deep down he realizes he didn't do that – he didn't report the abusers, report their wrong behavior, or be courageous in exposing his assailants' prejudice."

Hassan and Tariq both nodded, as if this made sense.

Amir added. "It's difficult to get someone to process things they have buried for so long. But maybe your father can be convinced that Omar is brave, that he's facing prejudice head-on, and that this is not the easy way out. At the moment, Omar triggers your father's shame. Maybe there's a way to trigger his admiration and his sense of indignation – to help him see Omar as brave and defiant in the face of prejudice. Let's go inside and see what's going on."

As they walked indoors, they noticed Hakim and Nassen were drinking coffee in the kitchen. They all walked in. Hakim stood and offered to pour cups for them.

Amir and Nassen stared at each other. Nassen cleared his throat and said, "Amir, I'm sorry." He didn't elaborate.

Amir put his hands on his brother's shoulder and said, "I'm sorry for what you've had to deal with over the years. Hopefully, we can all support one another."

Nassen nodded.

Hakim smiled as he realized he had averted a major rift in the family. They sat facing each other, largely in silence, sipping their warm cups of coffee. At some point, Tariq said, "I guess we'd better get to work."

Everyone nodded, stood, emptied their cups, and walked out onto the garage floor to begin work.

19

Chapter Nineteen - Cambridge

Omar sat at a long table in a conference room surrounded by tall windows with views of the Charles River and the skyline of Boston glowing in the orange light of the late afternoon sun. Three people sat opposite him, taking notes. They were young, recent star graduates of MIT. One was a woman, Indian. The other two were men — one from the States and the other from Mexico.

"Doctor Aziz, we are delighted you have reconsidered our offer," the Mexican began, glancing at his notes and looking up warmly at Omar.

"Call me Omar, please."

"Omar, we haven't found anyone with the same expertise as you have, and we would love to leverage your connections to form a partnership with Laval University. Given the support of the Quebec government, we think this could be lucrative in the long run."

"That might be difficult. The Moroccans have already reached out to them."

"Yes, we realize that. But isn't it the case that Morocco was able to make that connection through you? If you are here, might Laval reconsider and be open to overtures from the United States?"

"I don't know. Mohammed University and the company in Rabat had hoped to leverage its French and Arabic connections, creating a collaborative between Canada and the Middle East. They might find someone else with similar credentials and make it happen anyway."

"With all due respect, that's unlikely," the Indian woman said, alluding to Omar's unique background and expertise.

Omar blushed and shifted nervously, aware of the expectations being placed on him.

The interviewer from the States added, "It might not be too late. Are you aware of any agreements that were signed yet?"

Omar shook his head.

The Indian woman continued, "We think if you were to join our team, we could approach Laval to collaborate with us. We imagine the opportunity to become part of the network here – MIT, Harvard, BU, Northeastern, and Wentworth would be quite tempting."

"My mentors seemed to light up when I mentioned the possibility of teaming up with MIT."

"Whatever resources you need to get them to agree to that, we can provide."

Omar nodded.

"We've also discussed compensation. Although your position will be housed in the university, the project is supported by venture capital. You will teach and lead the research team."

One of the interviewers pushed a sheet of paper toward Omar and said, "The details of our offer are outlined here in the prospectus. Salary, insurance, and other benefits."

Omar glanced at the figures briefly. He tried to contain his excitement. He took some additional time to review the numbers, not wanting to appear too eager. He leaned forward and said, "Thank you for your offer and the opportunity. I accept."

The three interviewers looked at each other with surprise. They stood, smiled warmly, and reached their hands across the table to Omar. "Welcome. We know you will do a great job, and we hope you will be happy here in the Boston area."

"I'm sure I will," Omar said.

The team accompanied Omar down the hall and introduced him to human resources, where some preliminary paperwork was taken care of just before the end of the workday. The university would take care of securing Omar's working visa. He would begin teaching in the Spring semester, but the research project was already underway, and he would have only two weeks to move to Boston. He would use his time in Quebec to meet with counterparts at Laval University.

Omar was wild with excitement. The disappointment around leaving Rabat and the labored coming-out to his family were fading. He felt energized and encouraged that his life might be actually moving in a good direction, that the fates were not cruel. He called for an Uber and returned to his hotel at Boston harbor. He texted his parents and Hakim to share the good news.

He gazed out the window of his hotel at the harbor. The lights of East Boston and Logan Airport reflected off the choppy water. As he peered across the expanse, he thought of Morocco on the other side of the Atlantic and the journey his parents made to North America to start a new life. He was walking in their footsteps, only now he was making his way to the United States. It was ironic that given the hostility to Arabs and Muslims in the States, he felt finally safe, able to be himself as a gay man. He was encouraged by the diversity of the interviewers and realized he was part of a changing

demographic. He felt encouraged that he could integrate his ethnicity, faith, and sexual identity into a rich and satisfying life.

He hadn't spent much time in Boston, but he could imagine
moving into a pleasant apartment along the waterfront – perhaps in
one of the restored wharfs of the North End or in a new high-rise in
the Seaport District. His head spun with the logistical practicalities
of setting up a home.

It was a chilly November night. He vacillated between the desire
to call room service for dinner and the urge to go to the nearby
North End and celebrate at an Italian restaurant. He put on a heavy
coat, scarf, and gloves and headed outside.

Omar walked along the waterfront toward the North End. The
wind off the water was bitter, and he was eager to find a warm place
to eat. He walked up Richmond Street and peered into the restaurant where he and Brian had eaten and had been seen by Tariq and
Hassan months before. He felt a knot in his stomach, a reminder
of the mess he had made with Brian. It was early. There weren't too
many people inside yet, so he pushed open the door. The maître d'
greeted him and showed him a table.

He ordered some wine and appetizers. His parents responded to
his earlier text, elated by the news. They were excited he would be
nearby. Omar scrolled through some emails and checked a few messages. He set his phone down and took a long sip of wine. He looked
around the room and felt a rush of sensations wash over him. It was
an odd feeling, almost as if the aroma of the wine and the flavor
of the mushroom crepes he had ordered recreated the setting with
Brian nine months earlier. He could almost feel his presence. It was
uncanny, eerie. He fully expected him to walk up behind him, place
his hand on his shoulder, and lean down and give him a kiss.

He looked over his shoulder. There was no one.

He was tempted to text Brian but felt embarrassed. He had

walked away from him in Montreal and pushed forward with his move to Rabat. He had begun an intense relationship with Ibrahim and the only reason he was here now was that he had been caught, his duplicity impossible to hide. It felt opportunistic to reach out to Brian. It wasn't fair to treat him as a backup plan, as an afterthought.

He took his time eating the savory crepes and sipping the luscious wine he splurged on in celebration. He glanced at the menu and eyed several options for a main course. As he reached for his glass of wine, his hand brushed the side of his phone. He picked it up and said, "Oh, what the hell. I want to talk with him."

He composed a text. He vacillated between something formal and something clever. He hoped a bit of levity would be appreciated even if he had been a jerk in not keeping in touch with Brian. He typed and sent his message: "The view of Richmond Street is charming, but it's missing someone."

Brian's phone pinged as Omar's message arrived. Brian was having drinks with friends in the Seaport District of the city. His jaw fell as he read the text. He hadn't heard from Omar since Montreal. He realized he was just on the other side of the harbor. He showed the text to his friend Rita, whose eyes widened.

"That's the one from Quebec, right? Omar?"

Brian nodded.

"What does he want?"

"That fucker!" Brian exclaimed, cocking his head back in a gesture of indignation. "He can't do that."

"What, dear?" Rita asked.

"He can't just show up and hope to hook up with me. It doesn't work that way." Brian took a long sip of wine and looked out of the window at the dark water outside.

"What do you mean?"

"He's in Morocco, presumably with a wife or fiancé and living his fake devout Muslim life."

"Maybe not. Maybe things have changed."

"I doubt it. He's probably here for a conference or meeting. I won't play this game – as much as I would love to," he said, raising his brows.

Omar could see Brian had received and read the text. There was no response.

He typed a second message: "I have some good news."

Brian's phone pinged. He held it up to Rita, who smiled. Brian said, "He's probably going to announce he's getting married. I'm going to vomit," he said as he dramatically inserted two fingers into his mouth.

"Why would he want to tell you that? It must be something else."

Rita's comment aroused Brian's curiosity. He started to type a response and then erased it.

Omar typed another message. "Brian, I'm in town. Can we talk?"

Brian's body longed for Omar, and he could almost smell his skin and feel the solidity of his body pressed up against his. "What should I do?" he asked Rita.

"Go. See what he wants to talk about."

Brian looked off into the distance, deep in thought. He didn't want to sit through a long conversation about sexuality, religion, and traditions. He was tired of processing.

"I don't know. I'm not up for it."

"But you told me how much you loved him. I've never heard you use that word."

"It's over."

Rita could see in Brian's eyes that it wasn't over. He continued to medicate himself with work, alcohol, and quick tricks. The mere mention of Omar changed his countenance. He was irritated, but she could see a glow on his face.

"Go see what he wants. What do you have to lose?"

"A nice evening with you and your friends."

"You'll be distracted all night. Leave us be. Go see what he wants."

"Where are you?" Brian typed a message to Omar.

"At the Vinoteca. Tariq and Hassan aren't around. In fact, their bite has been muzzled."

When Omar's text arrived, Brian raised his brow. "Hm," he murmured. "Something's up."

"Go!" Rita said.

Brian put on his coat, dropped a few twenties on the table, and headed out onto the street. He called an Uber and, in a few minutes, was standing in front of the restaurant. Omar was sitting near the window, looking at his phone. The glow of the screen cast a soft light on his face. His eyes were alluring as ever.

Brian walked in, nodded toward Omar's table, and the maître d' gestured that he could proceed. Brian walked up unnoticed to Omar, who eventually glanced his way, undoubtedly sensing his presence. A large, warm smile formed on his face. He stood up and embraced Brian warmly. "I didn't think you would come."

"I wasn't going to," Brian said coldly, trying to conceal the excitement he felt standing so close to Omar. Omar returned a look of concern.

"Some wine?" he offered as they settled into their chairs, facing each other at the intimate table.

Brian nodded. The server came with another glass and poured him some. Brian lifted his glass to Omar's, and they said, "À notre santé."

"You look good," Omar began, peering into Brian's hazel eyes. He scrutinized them for some warmth, for a slight opening, a door through which he might enter and pick up where they left off.

Brian fought the urge to leap across the table and devour the luscious man in front of him. He was still resentful, angry, and wanted Omar to feel his pain. He stared at Omar and nodded. "You look good, too," he said with little warmth.

Omar felt Brian's prickliness. He wondered if he had made a mistake in reaching out to him. He decided to make one more effort and said, "For what it's worth, I'm sorry."

"For what?" Brian replied curtly.

"For not keeping in touch."

"I'm sure you were busy getting things set up in Morocco. How is that going?"

Omar looked across the room evasively. Brian detected Omar's nervousness and hesitation and wondered what might follow.

Omar turned his head toward Brian. He thought it would be thrilling to share the news of his new job with Brian, but, as he tried to formulate the words, he felt choked with emotion. He felt shame. He was perplexed. He just landed a lucrative position with the premier scientific university of the world. Why wasn't he elated?

"I have a new job," was all he could manage to say.

"Did they promote you?"

Omar shook his head. His eyes watered.

Brian sensed something portentous. He remained guarded.

"I fucked things up," Omar began.

"What happened?"

"I was caught having an affair with a male graduate student. They gave me an ultimatum – bring back a wife or return to Quebec for good."

Brian raised his brows. He was taken aback. He hadn't expected that bit of news, although it wasn't entirely surprising given the circumstances. "I take it if you have a new job, you must have told them *allez vous faire foutre.*"

Omar chuckled nervously at Brian's profanity and nodded. Brian took a deep breath. He realized whatever Omar's story, it was going to be interesting and full of surprising twists and turns. He relaxed his stern demeanor a little, reached his hand over to Omar's, and said, "Tell me what happened."

Omar felt the warmth of Brian's hand. Encouraged, he began, "I returned home. Lara and I met. I couldn't marry her, and I explained why. She was understanding and grateful."

"That's good," Brian said, realizing things were moving in a good direction.

"The big hurdle was my family."

Brian leaned back in his chair and braced himself.

Omar recounted his meeting with Hakim, his coming out to his aunts and uncles, and the long conversation he had with his parents. Omar's face relaxed, his breath slowed, and color returned to his face.

"Wow!" Brian exclaimed at the end of the account.

"So, what's the new job?"

"Well, when I was here last winter, a new company in Cambridge was interviewing me. When I decided not to go back to Morocco, I contacted them. They were still interested and, well, they offered me a position."

"So, you're moving to Boston?" Brian asked with furrowed brows. He was now certifiably alarmed. He had organized the last months of his life around his anger and the conviction that he was right all along. Work, alcohol, and lots of anonymous sex were the path to a happy existence. He now realized he was going to have to reassess things.

Omar nodded, visibly more animated. He reached for his glass and took a long sip. "Yes," he finally said with strength and force. "I'm moving to Boston, to the States."

"Congratulations," Brian said unconvincingly.

Omar sensed Brian's reserve. His eyes lacked the luminescence he had remembered from before. Where they had been aglow with eagerness and longing, they were now puzzled and mystified. Omar wanted to excuse himself and slip out the back door. He wondered if Brian had moved on, if he had made a mistake in presuming that he would be delighted to see him.

In an effort to buy some time to regroup, Omar asked, "Should we order?"

"I'm not that hungry. Maybe a plate of pasta. Something simple," Brian said.

Omar waved the waiter over and said, "I think we're ready to order."

The waiter looked at Brian. "I'll have a simple spaghetti with crushed tomatoes and a house salad."

"I'll have the veal chop," Omar added, folding the menu closed.

The waiter left, and Omar played nervously with his fork. "So, how have you been?" he asked.

"Great," Brian lied without elaboration.

Omar took a long sip of wine. Brian wasn't looking at him, and he felt like things were slipping out of his fingers. After coming out to his family, Omar felt emboldened. No more hesitation. He said, "Brian, the biggest mistake I made was walking away from you in Montreal that night. I have repeated the scene in my head countless times, and have wondered how I could change it, redo it, rewrite scene."

Brian's eyes watered. Omar was surprised.

Brian said nothing. He couldn't speak. But his eyes changed. Even behind the tears, they glimmered. Instead of darting nervously, they began to focus. They were warm and gentle. In them, Omar saw the eyes of a teenager who wondered why he wasn't lovable. Omar realized his walking away from Brian on that cold night in the Old Port of Montreal must have stirred painful memories.

Omar strained to find words that would console Brian. Everything he considered felt trite, shallow, cliché. He stared at Brian.

Brian felt the intensity of Omar's beautiful deep brown eyes, the imagination and idealism of an immigrant who wanted to make his mark. "You were following your dream," he said thoughtfully.

"I know, but my dream was to integrate Islam with science, to restore the golden age of Islamic scholarship. All I did was discover its fissures and my own cowardice."

"I don't see a coward," Brian said, surprised at his words. Deep down, he was impressed that Omar had come out to his family. He couldn't imagine that had been easy. "You faced the guardians of Islamic fundamentalism head on," Brian noted. "Either you're braver than you think or exceedingly reckless."

"Reckless," Omar said immediately, chuckling.

Brian shook his head. "No. Given what I know of Hakim, there was every reason to be hopeful they would ultimately come around. Nevertheless, it took courage."

Omar blushed.

Brian now wondered if he had the courage to take the next step. He had let his heart love again, and Omar had walked away. Was he being foolish to even consider another round?

"So, this student in Rabat?"

"Over."

Brian squinted his eyes, searching for assurance.

"Really."

"Did you love him?"

Brian's question startled Omar. Omar looked away evasively, gathering his thoughts. He turned to Brian and said boldly, "I thought so. In retrospect, I realized I was settling. He was smart, but he was engaged. We had a lot of clandestine sex, and it was exciting. But he didn't make my heart pound, my pulse race, or my skin warm. Only one person has done that." Omar looked intently into Brian's eyes.

Brian felt like he was going to explode. He wanted to say the same thing, but he held back.

"Can we start over?" Omar continued, looking imploringly at Brian with his irresistible eyes.

Brian paused, fighting competing responses in his head. Omar's shoulders contracted in apprehension. Brian leaned forward with his hands nestled together, deep in thought. Omar recoiled slightly in fear. Brian was about to say something, leaning forward forcefully. Suddenly, he reached his hand up and placed it behind Omar's neck and pulled him forward. He opened his mouth and gave Omar a long, deep, and warm kiss.

Omar kissed him back. Each clung tenaciously to the other, savoring the softness of their lips. Omar pulled back and whispered, "I take it that is a yes."

Brian blushed and nodded.

20

Chapter Twenty - Back in Quebec City

Brian glanced out of the window at the falling snow. It was an early snowfall, the first of the season. Large flakes danced through the air, covering rooftops and the stone ridge of the upper city rising above the hotel. Through the thick swirling whiteness, he could make out the outline of the apartment he and his buddies had rented nine months before on the Rue des Remparts.

He was awakened by the click of the door. Omar had gone out to retrieve a tray of croissants and coffee from the lobby of the hotel. He set the tray on the bedside table, sat down on the mattress, and pressed his seat up against Brian's side. "Time to get up," he whispered in Brian's ear. Brian had closed his eyes, pretending to be asleep.

Omar rubbed his hands over Brian's shoulder. His skin was soft and warm. He ran his hand up the back of Brian's neck and ran his fingers through his hair.

Brian rolled over and gazed into Omar's eyes, hovering over him. They were full of excitement and anticipation. Brian held his hand and could feel the confidence and resolve that were absent months earlier. He let the warmth of Omar's hands settle into his heart and soften the reticence that continued to surface from time to time.

"*Un café?*" Omar asked.

"*Oui, merci. Et ensuite, toi?*"

"I didn't know I was on the menu."

"You're always on the menu," Brian said, rubbing his hands over Omar's thighs.

Omar picked up one of the flakey chocolate croissants, pulled off a piece, and plopped it into Brian's mouth.

"How do they make these so good here? They are unbelievably delicious," Brian said as he savored the croissant.

"Lots of butter."

Brian smiled. He reached around Omar's waist and pulled him playfully towards him, on top of him. Omar arched back over the top of Brian's chest. Brian slid his hands inside Omar's shirt and felt the soft, warm, and hairy outlines of his chest. He could feel his heartbeat just below his hand. The solidity of his body felt reassuring. Life was no longer tenuous. It felt anchored, secure, coherent.

Brian nuzzled his nose in the back of Omar's neck and breathed in his distinctive scent, a mélange of caramel, chocolate, and toasted coffee. He nibbled on Omar's ear. Omar moaned and turned toward Brian, giving him a long, warm, moist kiss.

"Are you ready?" Omar asked Brian, peering into his hazel eyes.

Brian nodded. "Are you?"

"*Je crois que oui.* As ready as I will ever be."

Omar sat back up, and Brian asked, "When are they expecting us?"

"For a late lunch. They know we must get back to Boston tonight."

Brian glanced out at the snow. "Will the roads be okay? You know me and Quebec storms!"

"The first snow is never that problematic. The pavement is still warm. We'll be fine."

Brian leaned up on his elbows, took another sip of coffee, and nibbled on the croissant. Omar was looking out of the window, deep in thought. Brian had been reading up on theoretical physics and was intrigued by new models of energy. There was something calming, reassuring, and soothing in Omar's presence. Did the body really emit some kind of energy or aura? Was it possible to absorb someone else's vibrations? Could someone's positive presence heal? He had never felt better. He was less compulsive, drank less, and worked harder. He had fewer episodes of rage, anger, resentment. He had even pondered the idea of reaching out to his own parents. Could someone's presence do all that?

"What are you going to wear?" Brian asked.

"Casual – jeans and a pullover."

"And your parents?"

"Casual, too."

"Are you sure?"

"Yes. Don't worry. They will love you. Besides, I already laid out some things for you," he said as he looked across the room at the dresser.

Brian raised his brows. "I'm quite capable of dressing myself."

"I know. You're the sartorial genius."

"What did you lay out?"

"Well, there are those dark jeans that showcase your assets so nicely!"

"Omar, we're going to see your parents. I'm the nightmare that keeps them up. We don't have to make them more uncomfortable."

"I've matched the jeans with a nice oxford cotton shirt and a zipper sweater – a little conservative, but it has a nice European cut to it. I found it yesterday when we were out shopping."

Brian looked into Omar's eyes and smiled. He had quickly learned not to get in the way of his determination. It also felt re-assuring that Omar was so thoughtful and solicitous. Slowly, Brian had begun to trust that his affection and attention were authentic and likely to endure. His eyes were full of warmth and the touch of his skin familiar. Ever since Brian brought Omar home just a few weeks ago, and they had been inseparable.

"All joking aside. Seriously. How do you think this will go?" Brian asked.

"They can't wait to meet you."

"Didn't I meet them at the airport last winter?"

Omar nodded. A pained look dimmed the warmth of his face.

"A lot has transpired since then. It's hard to believe," Brian con-tinued. He took hold of Omar's hand and squeezed it tightly. Each felt apprehensive yet hopeful, taking turns reassuring each other.

Omar was relieved Brian was willing to forgive him, and never looked back. Brian was the perfect companion, one who understood his religious and scientific background and made his heart pound and pulse race. He couldn't wait for his parents to get to know Brian, and he hoped they would react to him the same way Hakim had.

Omar stood and asked, "I'll take a shower first?"

"There's not room for two?" Brian asked, raising one of his brows.

Omar glared at Brian, who quickly tossed the sheets and blan-kets to the side and got out of bed. His hair was tousled and his sex slightly stiff. For someone who loved to give the appearance of being fragile, colorful, and outrageous, his body had a gravitas to it. He was taut, lean, and muscular, with broad shoulders, thin waist, and thick glutes. He walked toward the bathroom defiantly, daring Omar to follow.

Omar heard Brian turn on the shower. He walked toward the bathroom and peered around the door. Brian was standing in the steamy shower and, as he saw Omar's face at the door, waved him in.

"I'll wait," Omar replied bashfully.

Brian pushed the shower door open, walked toward Omar, and took his hand, and dragged him into the shower. "*Mais, je suis habillé,*" Omar protested.

"Well, we'll have to take care of that," Brian suggested, pulling down Omar's wet sweatpants and fondling his balls.

They kissed. The warm water felt comforting, both still a little nervous about the impending luncheon. Brian lifted Omar's wet tee-shirt and kissed the edges of his pecs. Omar became aroused.

Omar was slowing shedding the shame and inhibitions about being a gay man. Sex didn't have to be something one stumbled into unintentionally. It didn't have to be something one did clandestinely, under false pretenses, or under the guise of having been seduced. It was something beautiful, a way to express love, affection, intimacy. Letting Brian caress his body was difficult. It meant accepting that he was handsome, lovable, desirable.

Brian, in turn, fought his own demons. He loved to seduce, to arouse, to be coy, and flirtatious. What he struggled with was imagining the body before him as companion, friend, lover. He feared that after a while, Omar would discover his shallowness and flee to someone deeper, more complex, and better boyfriend material.

As Brian stroked Omar's flesh and felt the contours of his sex, he gradually began to accept the idea that he was home, that this was the one who would love him back, embrace him as he was, and heal the dark gaps that haunted him and hardened his heart. He was ready to silence the chatter in his head and imagine a new script.

Brian and Omar soaped each other's bodies, washing away years of shame they held onto. They reached into each other's deepest contours and cavities, making sure each was ready for the next adventure. Both were aroused. Brian loved the soft but thick feel of Omar's sex as it hardened. Omar, in turn, loved to stroke the erect and stiff shaft Brian proudly projected in front of him. But neither felt inclined to bring the moment to a climax. They were too focused on the impending luncheon with Omar's parents.

After rinsing, their bodies glowed, and they smiled contently at each other. Omar reached for a thick towel and began to dry his partner. Brian relished Omar's affection, attention, and care. The shield around his heart was melting.

They dressed, packed, and checked out of the hotel. The valet brought them their SUV, filled with Omar's belongings. There was still room to pack more things stored at his parent's home. They scraped off the snow on the windshield and headed down the Boulevard Chaplain along the St. Lawrence River, retracing the steps Brian had taken with Omar's uncle earlier in the year.

The snow had stopped by the time they pulled into Omar's neighborhood. The street was covered in a thin layer of ice and devoid of cars, and Omar pulled into his parent's driveway. He noticed his mother's face hidden in the folds of lace covering the front window.

"*On y va?*" Omar asked.

"*Courage!*" Brian exclaimed.

Brian and Omar smiled at each other. Brian squeezed Omar's hand.

They walked up the driveway, knocked, and then pushed their way inside. Amir and Nebila were standing in the foyer as if they had been waiting for them both to arrive. Both were calm and smiling, their arms wrapped around each other. As Omar walked inside, they outstretched their arms and embraced him warmly.

Omar gave them each an embrace and kiss. He turned toward Brian and said, "*Ma et pa, c'est Brian. Brian, mes parents, Amir et Nebila.*"

Everyone replied, "*Enchanté.*"

Amir took their coats, and Nebila did something unexpected. It was a bold gesture, one that presaged the kind of future she imagined. She took Brian's hand, squeezed it warmly, and said, "Come. Let's go sit in the parlor."

She glanced back proudly over her shoulder at Omar and Amir, grinning. Brian's heart skipped a beat. He wondered if Omar had noticed. Brian concealed his own grin, not wanting her to think he was startled by her intimate act. In Nebila's hand, he imagined his own mother pushing past her discomfort and embracing her son with affection. His heart raced with excitement.

Nebila had made some appetizers and set them out colorfully on the coffee table. "*Vous voulez un café ou bien du thé?*" she asked Brian directly.

"*Café, merci. Et vous pouvez me tutoyer,*" he interjected. "We're going to be family."

Brian's invitation for Nebila to speak to him in the familiar voice was not unexpected. But Omar flinched when Brian suggested they would be family. It was all surreal, unimaginable.

Amir didn't flinch. He sat down next to Brian and began amiably, "Omar says you are a research scientist in Boston. What kind of research do you do?"

Brian enumerated some of his projects. Amir nodded, impressed with the breadth of Brian's expertise. Brian concluded, "It's nothing compared to what Omar is about to begin at MIT. He's a star already."

Amir beamed. Nebila returned from the kitchen with coffees. She poured each a cup and passed plates of Moroccan appetizers to each. They chatted, detailing Omar's new work.

"And Omar says you have been very gracious in welcoming him to your place," Nebila said.

Brian blushed and then looked at Omar, saying, "It's been something I've wanted to do for a long time. I'm happy he is there."

"Do you have any photos of the apartment?" Amir asked Omar.

Omar opened his phone and showed pictures of Brian's condo. Amir's and Nebila's eyes widened as Brian described the place, its location, and the amenities of the building.

"Will there be enough room for your things?" Nebila asked, looking over at a stack of boxes Omar was going to take to Boston.

Omar nodded. "Yes, there's plenty of room. In fact, there's a guest room. You'll have to come visit!"

Amir and Nebila looked at each other and beamed. Amir asked, "And how far is it from your work?"

"It's a quick subway ride. I could even walk in good weather."

They continued to talk about Boston and the new work. Then Nebila invited everyone into the dining room for dinner. The table was set with platters of lamb, couscous, and grilled vegetables. "*Nebila, c'est un banquet, une veritable fête,*" Brian said, amazed at the feast set out before him.

Amir cleared his throat as they took their seats. He invoked a blessing in Arabic and ended it in French. "*À notre nouveau beau-fils. Bienvenue dans la famille.*"

Omar gulped, coughed, and reached for a glass of water, taking a long sip.

"*Papa, c'est un peu prématuré,*" he said, protesting his father's use of the term son-in-law.

Amir nodded. "I don't think it's premature. You are both perfect for each other. I see it in your eyes, in the glow of your skin, in the warmth of your smiles. I've never seen you so at peace, son. It's a sign of Allah's blessing."

Omar coughed again. He never imagined hearing his father refer to his relationship with a man as a blessing from God.

"*Vraiment*," Amir added emphatically, wanting to make sure they knew he was serious.

Omar placed some lamb and couscous on his plate and passed the platter to Brian, who followed suit. They all loaded their plates and began to eat.

Omar hesitated, but then asked, "Dad, what happened? Where is all of this good will coming from?"

Amir cleared his throat, took a sip of water, and began, "I have been thinking. Your grandfather Khalid was a good man. But I always wondered why there wasn't a spark between him and Aisha. After Hakim's story the other day, I now know why. It always bothered me. They seemed like the perfect couple and we, the perfect family. But there was a degree of love and affection missing. Times have changed. It is possible for a gay man to find love and happiness in our society. I never told you this, but one of our suppliers is gay. He and his husband have two children. They adopted them. I have watched Vincent's family grow over the years. It is beautiful, and the kids are happy and smart and respectful."

Omar's eyes watered. In his wildest dreams, he never imagined his father encouraging him to form a gay partnership and have children. He glanced over at his mother. She was beaming.

"So, Brian, when might we meet your parents?" Amir asked.

Omar's face turned ashen, and Nebila noticed. She placed her hand on Amir, who looked at his son and then at Brian. "*Je suis désolé.* Did I say something wrong?"

Omar looked at Brian, who was choked with emotion. Brian nodded, and Omar said, "Brian's parents kicked him out of the house when he was 17. He hasn't seen them since."

"*C'est pas possible.* A parent can't do that," Amir said thoughtfully.

"They did," Omar reiterated.

"You're always welcome in our family," Amir said emphatically.

A few tears streaked down Brian's face. Nebila stood and refilled his glass of water. He took a sip.

"*Merci beaucoup.* It means a lot."

They all ate in silence for a while.

Eventually, Amir asked about Omar's efforts to connect Laval University with the new research in Boston. They continued visiting, sticking to safe topics of work, apartment, travel. They had dessert and coffee. Omar then looked at his watch and said, "We should be going. We will have a long drive to Boston."

Everyone stood, embraced, and kissed. Brian and Omar bundled up for the cold outside. They loaded the car with more boxes and returned to give Amir and Nebila another hug each. They walked back outside, got into the car, and drove off.

Between Sherbrooke and the border, Brian pointed out the place where he had skidded off the road last winter. Once in Vermont, Brian smiled as he noticed the peaks of the mountains white with the first snowfall. He looked forward to skiing with Omar and visiting his future in-laws. He was deep in thought, and Omar assumed he was nursing old wounds. Omar reached over and took Brian's hand. "I'm sorry my father touched a raw nerve regarding your parents."

"It's okay. I can't believe how welcoming and loving they were."

"Yes. Even I was surprised and taken aback. I knew they had softened, but I never imagined they would have been so effusive and warm."

"They are amazing!" Brian repeated. "It makes me wonder about my own. If fundamentalist Muslims can embrace a gay son, even embrace the idea that their gay son might marry and have children, why can't a fundamentalist Catholic couple do the same?

Omar glanced over at Brian and nodded, waiting for him to continue.

"Once we get established in Boston, I think I'm going to reach out to my parents."

"That's courageous," Omar said, looking at Brian with wide eyes.

"I'm in a different place. Between their rejection and Eric's betrayal, I went into a dark place. I don't think I believed I was lovable. You've changed all that."

Omar smiled. "I'm afraid I didn't do a very good job of it at first."

"We never know what people have gone through, what scars they are carrying in their bodies, and how the wounds sabotage their relationships. You helped me realize all that I was doing to mask the pain. I'm not going to do that anymore."

"I'm proud of you," Omar said.

"So, your dad mentioned children," Brian noted, shifting subjects.

Omar gulped. He gripped the steering wheel tightly. "Did he? I don't recall."

"I think you do. What would you think of a little Omar?"

"First of all, I don't believe in having children outside of marriage."

"That's easily rectified, particularly in Boston or Quebec. And what's the second problem?"

"None."

Brian took a deep breath, leaned back in his seat, and looked out of the front window. Everything seemed so surreal – the snowy mountains, memories of a frightening accident, the intrigue of Morocco, and now an affable and handsome companion sitting inches from him. Omar was alien – a North African, Muslim, and francophone. He came from an extended family and clan that were insular and protective of each other.

The brief amount of time Brian and Omar had spent together added to the dreamlike quality of the moment. They had only met months ago, yet Brian sensed a deep and enduring connection, perhaps one that had roots in a past life or simply drew from their common perspectives – a terrain waiting to be explored and excavated.

Omar stared out onto the highway. He was driving the car, but his thoughts were swirling with impressions of Quebec City, Sherbrooke, and Rabat. He recalled the drive he and Brian took to Volubilis and the uncertainty he felt then about the choice to work in Morocco. In retrospect, the sequence of events all led to this moment, and they made sense – even the embarrassing ones. But, at the time, they were frightening and disturbing. He wondered how he could have been so deluded and misguided.

From time to time, he found himself fixated on minor things – Brian's shoes, the fabric of his shirt, the scent of his cologne, and style of his sunglasses. It was as if these details – as insignificant as they were individually – represented a portal into the mind of his companion. They were a collection of choices and decisions, small fragments of the personality of another person. At this point in their budding relationship, idiosyncrasies were charming and endearing and neither imagined they would be annoying. It was the honeymoon stage of their romance.

Their route passed through Franconia Notch and the dramatic view of Cannon Mountain. Its impressive ski slopes lined the highway. "You're going to take me skiing this year, right?" Omar interjected, as they snaked their way between the impressive peaks.

"How does Switzerland sound?"

"You're kidding," Omar replied, his eyes widening.

"I had made plans with Roberto, Carlos, and David," Brian noted. Omar gave him a worried look.

"The other day, I hinted to Roberto there could be a fifth person, and he started screaming over the phone. He was ecstatic about the news. He predicted back in February that you were the one."

228 - MICHAEL HARTWIG

"Really?"

"Yes. Once he was reassured that our friendship wasn't at risk, he recognized how perfect you were for me."

Omar continued to give Brian a scrutinizing look. Brian detected his incredulity and said, "Yes. Really. He's not as much of a jerk as he came off back in Quebec City. In fact, he already found us a larger rental in Grindelwald, with three bedrooms and three baths. No risk of an interloper. In fact, I wouldn't be surprised if he brings someone himself."

Omar sighed and let his shoulders relax. He was happy to be welcomed into a tight-knit group of friends, and the idea of skiing with Brian in the Alps was beyond his wildest dreams. "And this place – Grindelwald. What's it like? It sounds daunting."

"Relax. The runs are like those at Mont-Sainte-Anne. But the setting is dramatic. The ski runs face a range of glacier-studded peaks that are simply breathtaking. And, given the quick learning curve you've been on all year, I imagine you will not only ski like a pro, but will be turning heads as we line up for lifts."

Omar blushed.

"Exactly! I'm going to have to fight the locals off. Those killer eyes, luscious lips, muscular frame, and a few other assets we will keep hidden, are all mine! Remember that!"

Omar grinned. The mental tour of the Alps quickly gave way to the list forming in his head of what they needed to accomplish in the next couple of days. Moving to a new city so quickly was overwhelming. He looked over and scrutinized Brian, hoping he wouldn't detect any hesitation or regret at their decision to move in together. It had been an impulsive and hasty decision, but one they both seemed eager to embrace.

Brian turned and gave him a warm smile. No evidence of regret or vacillation. It was as if he had read Omar's thoughts. He said,

"I can't wait to get settled together in Boston." He glanced over his shoulder at the boxes they had picked up at Omar's parents' home.

"It's not too much?"

"Are you kidding? There's plenty of room, and this is a great opportunity to clear out some old things and buy some new stuff together."

Omar beamed.

The skyline of Boston eventually came into view with the soft orange light of sunset reflecting off the glass towers. A stream of red taillights led toward the downtown tunnel.

They made their way to the modern Seaport District, pulled up to Brian's building, and parked in the garage. They carried a few boxes with them and proceeded to Brian's unit. Once inside, they set the boxes down and turned on the lights. Brian turned toward Omar, took him by the shoulders and said with great affection and warmth, "Welcome home."

Omar leaned toward Brian and gave him a passionate kiss.

He then lifted his hand and dangled Brian's car keys in front of him. "I knew when I stood on your porch in Quebec City and said, *J'ai votre voiture*, that it was I who had lost traction and was skidding out of control. I felt like I was falling off a cliff when I first saw you."

Brian cocked his head in disbelief. "You always seemed calm, cool, and in control."

Omar shook his head. His eyes began to water.

Brian wiped his tears and traced his finger over Omar's brows and along the distinctive lines narrowing at his temples. He then took hold of his hands and said, "I promise I will always be there holding you firmly and catching you if you slip or fall."

Omar was moved by Brian's declaration and wanted to reply. He found it difficult to talk, as if he was on the verge of crying.

All he could manage to eke out was, "You are so beautiful – inside and out."

Omar's words were exactly what Brian needed to hear. They settled deep within his chest. He smiled and embraced Omar, rubbing his hands up and down his back.

At that moment, each sensed that time had stood still, that a constellation of events and circumstances had brought them together. Both let the scales of self-doubt fall. They could feel each other's affection and love. It was healing and reassuring. They both imagined there would be rough and slick patches ahead. But both felt confident as they stood on the threshold of Brian's apartment, ready and eager to embrace their future together.

The End (for now)

Author Information

Michael Hartwig is a Boston and Provincetown-based author of LGBTQ fiction. Hartwig is an accomplished professor of religion and ethics as well as an established artist. His original oil paintings are represented by On Center Gallery in Provincetown.

Hartwig grew up in Dallas but spread his wings early on – living in Rome for five years, moving to New England on his return, and then working in the area of educational travel to the Middle East and Europe.

His fiction weaves together his interest in LGBTQ studies, ethics, religion, art, languages, and travel. The books are set in international venues. They include rich local descriptions and are peppered with the local language. Characters grapple not only with their own gender and sexuality but with prevailing paradigms of sexuality and family in the world around them.

Hartwig has a facility for fast-paced plots that transport readers to other worlds. They are romantic and steamy as well as thoughtful and engaging. Hartwig imagines rich characters who are at crossroads in their lives. In many instances, these crossroads mirror cultural ones. There's plenty of sexual tension to keep readers on the edge of their seats, but the stories are enriched by broader considerations – historical, cultural, and philosophical.

Other Titles By Hartwig

Crossing Borders

Old Vines

Oliver and Henry

A Roman Spell (sequel to Oliver and Henry)

Our Roman Pasts

CPSIA information can be obtained
at www.ICGtesting.com
Printed in the USA
LVHW022231191122
733617LV00014B/730